FAMINE, WAR *and* *Love*

Stephen C. Joseph

For those who left All Else behind,

Turned faces towards the West,

To seek a Newer World

CONTENTS

HISTORICAL PROLOGUE

THE NETHERLANDS IN WW II

Following a series of diplomatic moves and counter-moves, Nazi Germany invaded Poland on September 1, 1939. France and Britain declared war on Germany two days later, in fulfillment of their treaty obligations to Poland. World War II had begun in Western Europe, though active ground combat was still some months away. This initial period is sometimes dubbed the 'Sitzkrieg', or the 'Phony War'.

On May 10, 1940, the Germans invaded France through Belgium and Luxemburg, striking with heavy armor through the Ardennes Forest and evading France's 'impregnable' Maginot Line. The defeat and capitulation of France followed in early June, and, suddenly, the British had evacuated Dunkirk, and the Germans were in Paris.

The Netherlands, a Parliamentary Monarchy headed by Queen Wilhelmina, had every reason to feel that their neutrality with Germany would be secure, as it had been during World War I, and restated by treaty as recently as 1939.

However, as part of their attack through the Low Countries in May, 1940, the Germans mounted a massive air bombing of the Dutch port city of Rotterdam, specifically attacking civilian areas rather than the industrial and port areas (which they wanted to spare as a base for their anticipated future invasion of Britain), followed up by parachute and land forces invasion.

Hopelessly outgunned and unprepared (with weapons mostly of WW1 vintage and an air force that consisted of more than 60% bi-planes) the Dutch government, threatened by Germany with a similar bombing of the city of Utrecht, surrendered within days. The Queen and Royal Family and a number of high elected officials escaped by sea to Britain, and the Germans installed a direct-authority military Government of Occupation.

During the next five years, the citizens of the Netherlands endured an extremely harsh and repressive Occupation. There had been, for almost a decade, an active but minority Dutch Nazi Party, and there were indeed significant instances of collaboration with the Germans, especially by the police, military, and civil authorities, as well as by individual citizens. But there was also widely-prevalent individual and organized resistance, both passive and quasi-military. The pre-war efficiency of the Dutch government's own information and social services systems was used effectively by the Nazis to enforce tight control.

In 1941, the Nazis began to round up Dutch Jews for deportation to the extermination camps. Despite the overt opposition of both the Dutch Catholic and Protestant Church hierarchies, and the extraordinary heroism of many individual families who hid and sheltered Jewish children and adults, more than 120,000 Dutch Jews were sent to the extermination camps, and less than 15 % survived.

There was also a Dutch Auxiliary' group that ferreted out Jews for the Nazis... for a price.

The Nazis also deported more than 500,000 Dutch men (about 15% of the Dutch male population) to work as slave laborers in German factories and in building defensive works.

Thus, in some sense the Netherlands under the Nazi Occupation may be thought of as a land divided against itself. It has been said that the estimated 140,000 people more or less directly involved with the Resistance were roughly balanced by about the same number who were more or less passively or actively compliant with the Occupation regime. But daily life under the Occupation of the Netherlands was a brutal affair of terror raids by day and by night, arbitrary street arrest, suppression of expression (including death penalties for possession of a radio set), and harsh rationing of food and most consumer goods.

The flat and largely-unforested and open landscape of the Netherlands increased the difficulty of maintaining effective military Resistance activities.

There were also extremely savage penalties for any infringement against the Nazi regime. In one notorious atrocity, in the small town of Putten, in early October, 1944, following the kidnapping of a German SS Officer by the Resistance, the SS shot 7 townspeople (including a teen-aged girl), took all 660 of the men of the town hostage, deported 589 of them to slave labor in Germany (of whom only 49 eventually returned alive; 5 of these died shortly after repatriation). The Germans then razed 87 of the 600 houses in the town.

THE HUNGER WINTER
(HONGERWINTER)

Following the Allied Normandy invasion of June, 1944, the Allied armies moved north and east, liberating Paris and thrusting through Belgium and the southern Netherlands. Their objective was to strike east across the Rhine River, using whatever number of railway bridges that could be captured before being destroyed by the retreating Germans, encircling the German industrial heartland of the Ruhr, and thence on to Berlin.

In early September, as the southern areas of the Netherlands fell to the Allies, the Dutch believed that total liberation of their country was near; there was even a 'Mad Tuesday' in the first week of September in which the civilian population poured into the streets in joy. Queen Wilhelmina sent a radio message from England, urging that the Dutch railway workers strike, to hinder military movements by the Germans as the Allies drove on. The workers responded, and rail traffic came to a halt.

The Germans were furious at this, and as a reprisal enforced a complete embargo of food supplies, fuel, and other materials necessary for survival, into Northern Holland, encompassing an area roughly north of the Wall River, and west of the Rhine. Food rationing had been severe throughout the Occupation, but now fell drastically, reaching a low of 1900 and then 500 calories per person per day. Normal daily caloric requirements for adults is 2,000-2,500. Five hundred calories represent two slices of bread, two small potatoes, and half a sugar beet. No added protein, no fats, no oils, no vitamins.

The Allies attempted a massive airborne and ground assault at Arnhem, dubbed "Operation Market Garden", which would have opened the way for the direct invasion of Germany, and the total liberation of the Netherlands, but the operation failed, and northern and eastern Netherlands remained in German hands throughout the winter and early spring.

And the winter of 1944-5 proved to be one of the coldest and longest on record. In November the canals froze over, closing what had been a trickle of contraband food imports into the area.

Starvation stalked the land. More than 19,000 people starved to death between November, 1944 and May, 1945. Infants and the aged were the most affected. Eighty percent of the deaths were among males, as husbands often provided for their wives and children first.

Thus that winter has been known thereafter by the Dutch as the *Hongerwinter*—the Hunger Winter. Later medical research has shown the persistence of effects of that period of starvation onto the infants born or conceived during the Hunger Winter, and perhaps even carrying over to a second generation.

By April of 1945 it had become clear that the War was headed to an inevitable conclusion, although Hitler had ordered total defense without surrender.

The Dutch appealed to the Allies for food relief, first to Eisenhower and to Churchill. It seems that Churchill played the strongest role in moving the Allies to a specific effort. He then wrote to Roosevelt, who may not have seen the correspondence in the day or two before his death on April 12, but the incoming President Truman did, and the Allies agreed that something must be done.

A daring proposal was made to the German Army of Occupation, through General Eisenhower: A one-off, time-limited, area-specific truce would allow Allied bomber aircraft to drop food supplies at very low altitude to the Dutch. No bombs would be dropped, and the Germans would with-hold anti-aircraft fire or assault by fighter aircraft during the drops. Food parcels would be dropped from as low as 400 feet altitude (the normal cruising and bombing flight altitudes of the bombers was between 10,000 and 29,000 feet)!

Perhaps surprisingly, the Germans agreed, and over a two-week period in April/May more than 11 million kilograms of food were dropped by British Lancaster and American B-17 Flying Fortress aircraft. The British called it "Operation Manna", and the Americans called it "Operation Chow Hound." Undoubtedly, thousands, perhaps tens of thousands, of lives were saved at the critical point of the late Hunger Winter. The Dutch people have never forgotten.

By the first week of May, the German occupation of the Netherlands was falling apart. The Russians had entered Berlin; the Allies were across the Rhine. Hitler had committed suicide on April 30. The Germans surrendered the Netherlands on May 5, and the war in Europe ended with the formal signing of a declaration of German Unconditional Surrender on May 8.

Immediately, large truck caravans of food relief, including significant contributions by the Canadian Army, who had fought their way into the Scheldt estuary towards Antwerp, added to the relief provided. The ground supply effort was known as Operation Faust.

The Hunger Winter was over, and life was slowly returning to normal. But the survivors themselves could never again be fully 'normal', as they carried within them the nutritional, physical, and psychological scars of the famine.

During the Chowhound airdrops, only three B-17 aircraft were lost, 2 in crashes and 1 with an engine aflame, which was allegedly the last B-17 to be lost in Europe during World War II. There were only a few reports of light-weapons ground fire directed at the planes.

Operations Manna and Chowhound may be said to have set part of a pattern for the later 1949 Berlin Airlift, this time with the Germans themselves as major beneficiaries, though in the latter case the planes were able to land instead of dropping supplies from the air.

THE 1980'S FAMINE IN ETHIOPIA

The Horn of Africa (currently Ethiopia, Somalia, Eritrea, and Djibouti) is home to some of the most ancient and fabled civilizations and empires known to history, with traditions and records going back as far as 3,000 B.C and perhaps even further. It has also been an area of constant conflict and warfare, among tribes, competing cultural aggregations, formal empires, religions, and warlords.

In 'modern' times, Mussolini's Italy invaded Ethiopia from a colonial base in then-Italian Somaliland and Eritrea in 1935, driving out the then-Emperor Haile Selassie, who then returned to his throne in 1941, annexing Eritrea in the process. In 1974, Selassie was dethroned and executed by a Marxist military group (the Derg), which itself became embroiled in a series of rebellions, local civil wars, banditry, and ongoing campaigns for independence by various factions (Eritreans, Somalis, Tigreans, etc.). During the "Red Terror" of government repression (1974-1978), tens of thousands were killed and political chaos ensued, with farmers driven off their land, and populations terrorized and victimized by one 'side' or another (or both). Food prices soared and food production fell, government policies of re-location and 'villageization' displaced millions, food supplies were confiscated and used as a weapon, and tens of millions of dollars were spent on weapons and military support of client groups by Cold War adversaries (Russia, Cuba, and the United States). The Derg finally fell in 1991, but not before the Ogaden war of 1977 led to the final independence of Somalia. Continued rebellion in Eritrea did not lead to its full independence until 1991.

By 1980, drought conditions in northern and central Ethiopia would have, in any case, resulted in hardship and hunger for the mainly subsistence small farmers and livestock-raising rural population. But a series of small (and not so small) wars, careless, corrupt, and brutal government decisions, and an initial lack of awareness, and neglect, of the situation by the rest of the 'world community', resulted in a series of linked famines that took the lives of up to 500,000 people. In truth, anything like a close accounting of the death toll, or a partition of it between 'simple' famine, human violence, and political chaos will never be known.

Perhaps the most-representative analogue to the Ethiopian famines of the 1980's would be the European Hundred Years' War of the 14th and early 15th Centuries, with its accompanying local famines and epidemics (e.g. the Black Death), and the decimation of civilian populations, in which up to twenty percent of the entire Western European population is estimated to have perished.

By 1985, the world became aware of the depth and chaos of the Ethiopian food situation, in large part because of the initial efforts of BBC and Canadian Broadcasting Company journalists, and then pop-music stars and entertainment entrepreneurs, who may be credited with having prodded the world media and political communities into remedial action. But in 1982 and 1983, the year of this part of the story, that was all in the future...

THE MAIN CHARACTERS

"Famine, War, and Love" is a novel of two families, across three generations, whose lives are woven together through two of the most dreadful politically-driven famines of modern times. The circumstances of the interactions of these individuals may seem at first as quite implausible coincidence. On deeper look, however, their story is an entirely conceivable peek at individual Destiny.

The main characters speak to us in their own voices, and project their own thoughts, as they would reveal them months, years, or even decades after the events described.

THE BRANDSMA-
VERMEER FAMILY

(Putten, Netherlands, and Toronto, Canada)

KAREL BRANDSMA ── BERTINE DE GROOT
(1880-1945)   m.   (1883-1975)

FREDDI BRANDSMA ── JACOB VERMEER
(1905-1985)   m.   (1900-1945?)

CHRISTINA VERMEER ── JOHN EVANS   BABY BOY VERMEER
(1932-)   m.   (1922-1968)   (1945-1945)

ELSA VERMEER-EVANS
(1954-)

Elsa Vermeer-Evans is the first-born in the New World to the Brandsma-Vermeer family, Dutch refugees from the Second World War. Born and raised in Toronto, Canada, she attends university, medical school, and becomes a pediatrician with special interests in child malnutrition and children in difficult circumstances. After a short stint in a remote Indian Health Zone in Canada, she arranges to go to Ethiopia in 1983 to work as a pediatrician in a famine relief camp near Hosaina in North-Central Ethiopia.

THE RILEY FAMILY

(Shawnee, Oklahoma, and Topeka, Kansas)

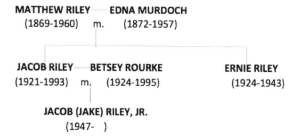

Jake Riley is the son of Jacob Riley and Betsey Rourke, who were married in 1946, immediately following Jacob, Sr.'s discharge from duty with the US Army Air Corps in Europe, where he was co-pilot of the B-17 Flying Fortress "Big Chief", and flew 30 combat missions over Europe. Only one in four B-17 crew members survived 25 missions. Jacob's son, Jake Riley, is a somewhat foot-loose and fancy-free long-distance truck driver and auto mechanic, who decides to follow his star and see the world. He arrives in Addis Ababa, Ethiopia, in late 1982.

PART ONE:
THE HUNGER WINTER

CHRISTINA VERMEER (1950)

I've just turned 18 years' old now, and sometimes when I try and look back at my childhood, I get terribly confused. One would think that a young person, looking back, would usually have a sense of continuity, of a life that flowed like a river, albeit one in which notable events or circumstances stood out like islands in that river of time. A special birthday, changes of location or family conditions, perhaps a very happy moment, or perhaps a very sad one. A child born into a loving and capable family, as I was initially, would, I think, have that kind of sense of his or her own life, and that in turn would provide a sense of security, of belonging, of safety in that gentle and welcoming world that childhood is 'supposed' to inhabit.

But it has not been that way for me. For me, I have a sense of very discontinuous episodes, almost like the separate lives of four separate, individual people. I would worry more about this than I do, except that when I have spoken about it with close friends of my own age, who have experienced the same bit of Dutch history that I have, they often confessed to similar feelings. I also tried to talk about it once, some two years ago, with my mother, Freddi, whom I love deeply, and with whom I have shared some of the most difficult things that life has to offer. She looked long and hard at me, said, "That is all right, Love, we all feel that way," and then she wept uncontrollably, something I had never see her do before, even in the most bitter of times.

I am not a timid person, not at all. I have a firm core inside me, that has carried me through each of my Second, Third, and Fourth lives so far, and which I know will carry me through those lives to come.

I omit my First Life, that one between my birth in 1932 and when I was eight years old, in 1940, and the Germans came and took my country. Of that First Life I remember virtually nothing—no events, no feelings, no anythings. Of course, I know that all children have initially inchoate, then progressively-conscious, memories of their first several years, but I have not only that inchoate stage, but one that lasted far longer, at least in my later conscious memory. Nothing. Absolutely nothing.

As I have pondered on this, I come to the conclusion that the stresses, uncertainties, terrors, and privations of my lives numbers Two and Three (the first four years of the Nazi occupation, when I was aged 8 through 11, and then the final year, the year of the Hunger Winter, when I was 12): that these have wiped that first slate clean. Effectively, the price of surviving Lives Two and Three has been to lose, forever, Life number One.

I don't know if that makes sense to anyone else, but it makes sense to me. The price of building the strong core that enabled me to survive Lives Two and Three, from 8 to 12 years of age, was to put away forever any trace of Life One, from birth to 8.

Life Two was the life of a child in an adult's hostile world, powerless to affect the flow of circumstances around her, no matter how hurtful or terrifying they might be. It was a life of accepting and enduring whatever the adult world around one would demand.

Life Three, that short but endless eight or nine months of the Hunger Winter, was when I realized it was all up to me, that only I could be mistress of my fate. That was when I became a woman, though still mostly in a child's body.

So, at least in faulty memory, my earliest conscious recollection was of the bombing of Rotterdam in early May of 1940. I doubt I actually heard or saw the explosions and fire, for our house was more than 40 kilometers away from the city, but the terror and shock of my parents, and of our neighbors, I can see in my mind's eye as if it were yesterday. I suppose it may be similar to what a dog experiences if indirectly exposed to a very violent scene of loud noise, physical threat, and anger, which leaves its effect more or less permanently on that dog's behavior.

And then the German soldiers were there, in our village, in our houses, in our streets and gardens and parks and playgrounds, and wherever else they wished to be. I don't remember their actual coming, but I will forever remember their being there, as if they always had been, and always would be.

And noise. The noise of shouted commands or challenges in the street. Of growling cars, motorcycles, armored vehicles, whose exhaust fumes and revving engine noise bounced back and forth between the narrow streets' stone walls of the village. Of boots and of flashlights that seemed to have a noise of their own, of fists banging on house doors and fierce dogs barking and pulling at the leash, or the breaking down of those doors, in the middle of the night, and of the weeping of people carried away. And of the weeping of the people left behind.

When I went to school, it was as if the presence of the Germans was there, actually in the classroom, the ghost of their threatening presence palpable to us, the children, and to our teachers alike. One learned to speak carefully, and one learned not to ask the wrong questions. One even learned to not dare look in the wrong direction, or with the wrong expression.

It was the same in the streets of the village, and in the shops, and even in the Churches. We learned from our elders to speak 'naturally' in a form of code, and this loss of honesty became, for all of us, a betrayal of our own character. And we learned to distrust each other, in the most fundamental ways. Not only those who collaborated in minor or major ways with the Nazis, but all of us, were in some ways corrupted, even the children.

And then there were the things which disappeared. The playground or park or town office which was suddenly off-limits. The streets and squares which were off-limits at night. The night itself, which disappeared under curfew. And most, most of all, our friends and neighbors and strangers who disappeared, dragged away after a night-time raid, vanished into thin air after being stopped in the street, some (often Jews) who vanished even before they vanished, who became invisible and silent, whether there or not.

And then even trust disappeared, because whom could one trust? What was in that sideways glance or nosy question from the smiling neighbor, or the stranger in the street, or the town official who sought preference from the Germans? How could one even trust oneself, when, by error or intent, disappearance lay just around the corner.

Perhaps the adults thought that we children did not sense nor experience these things. But that is not so. We did, and perhaps more acutely than adults did. For our fears, and nightmares, and terrors, were, if anything, less logical, less detailed, and less comprehensible than theirs. And thus, far greater.

But I fear I am getting a little ahead of myself. As far back as I can remember, we lived in a small stone and brick two-story house, outside the edges of the little village of Amersfoort, itself not very far from the town of Putten. My mother and I live there to this day, though we will soon leave it. Ours was a mix of village and rural life: next to our house was a small outbuilding, a sort of barn, you could call it, and between the house and the barn was our outdoor privy. The land area belonging to the house was mostly enclosed by wire fence, and we kept a vegetable garden, a milk cow, chickens, several goats, and usually one or two pigs. Our three bicycles (which later were to probably save our lives, or at least mine and my mother's) stood wherever was most convenient at the moment: in the barn or by the house.

Our house had running water, electricity, and cooking gas. Downstairs was a front entrance facing the road, a sitting-room/dining room with a good-sized fireplace and chimney, and a small but tidy kitchen. A back door from the kitchen led out to the privy, the small barn, and the 'farm' area.

At the side of the living/dining room was a narrow staircase leading to the upper floor, on which were located two bedrooms (one for my father and mother, and one for me), a 'spare bedroom' (for the brother or sister that I never had), and my mother's 'sewing room.'

Completing our homestead was our mixed-breed, vocal, and loveable dog, 'Highball' (named after the powerful locomotive engine, not the drink), and our mostly-invisible cat, 'Pumpkin.'

My mother was in charge of the house, the barn, the garden, the animals, and us.

My father, Jacob Vermeer, was a Section Manager on the Railroad. He loved his work, was evidently good at it, and seemed to me to be a natural leader of men, well-respected but not aloof. He was active in the Railway Workers' Union, and as I think about it now, was probably a Communist—but we Dutch didn't think so much about those things then, not until the Germans came. Later on, after they did, men used to come to the house on some nights, never more than 2 or 3 on a night, coming in always only one at a time, after it was dark, and sitting and talking quietly, without lights on or candles, smoking and talking. Then they would leave, quietly, and one at a time, the way they had come.

Thinking back on it now, I "knew but didn't know", and did not need to be told to never, ever, talk about it or even ask questions. My mother always went up to the sewing room when the men came at night, and I never heard her and my father discussing it.

Like every child in the Netherlands during the Occupation, my greatest fear, and the stuff of my most desperate nightmares, was that my father would be taken away by the Germans, snatched off the street and deported as a slave, or pulled from our arms during one of his night-time kitchen meetings. This fear was so great that I could never even ask my parents if it might happen.

Because we lived not far from the town of Putten, I was served, battered really, with a concrete example of that fear. I did not myself see the German raid on Putten, but I heard about it for weeks on end after the event. As the world now knows (unless it has forgotten), the Resistance kidnapped an SS Officer. In retaliation, the Germans shot 7 civilians, who may or may not have been members of the Resistance. It is unlikely that the 17 year-old girl who was among those murdered was. Then the Germans took all 600 adult males of the village captive, and sent 589 of them to slave labor in Germany. Finally, they burned some 80 houses in the village.

My father's work saw him often in Putten, as it was a minor headquarters on the railway line. Only good fortune (if that is what it was) had kept him out on the rail-line that day. Much later, after the war ended, we learned that only 49 of the men who were deported to Germany returned alive. Of course, by that time, my father was long gone, and my nightmares had been fulfilled.

When the Occupation began, I was eight years' old, and already well-along in the village primary school, a ten-minutes' or so walk from our house. Life seemed in many ways to go on as normal at first—at home, to and at school, at play with my friends. But of course nothing was normal, not in the street, not at school, not playing in the nearby fields or small woods, not at home, not chatting with neighbors or storekeepers. It was as if you were always living on two levels at once. One was how it 'seemed to be.' The other was an underlying reality, which as a child I only partially but not fully understood, which was how it 'really was.' So actions, words, and even private thoughts were never exactly what they were: they were both more and less, if you follow what I mean.

And then there would be one of those searing moments when the veils were stripped away, when the anger, hatred, resentment, aggression, fury, destruction, and above all the fear, would overwhelm the pretense, and then one would have to live with the consequences.

I think now that, perhaps, it was this experience of persistent simultaneous duality that caused me to see my own life as a series of non-continuous phases, of individual portraits rather than moving film.

I am not certain how many times as a child of the Occupation I actually spoke to a German soldier. It was certainly very few and each occasion very brief and one-sided. If a question or command was barked at you in the street, you put your head down, said as little as possible, and got away as quickly as you could. If a German came into the school-room, it was to talk with a teacher, and you kept your eyes glued to your own desk. If, in the most terrifying of instances, the Germans came to your house, you ran upstairs or to the barn if you could, and prayed your mother and father would still be there when the Germans left. If you saw adults being questioned, or arrested in the street, you looked the other way and walked the other way. And if you heard a night raid, or saw one next door, you hid yourself away so that you could see or hear no one, and no one could see or hear you.

There was no question of interaction, or even curiosity. A very, very, few of the older girls took up with a German soldier. That happened more in the big cities rather than in the small towns and villages like ours. As the privations and shortages became more and more acute with time, it happened more often, and when Liberation finally came, those girls had a very difficult, and sometimes violent, time, often having their heads shaved and painted, being paraded through the streets, and then shunned. But I never saw that in our village.

As the War went on, the other source of terror was, strangely, a result of the actions of the British and Americans, whom we knew were trying to rescue us. With the increasing frequency of massive Allied bombing raids into Europe came increasing destruction, deliberate or accidental, in both large cities and small towns. We did not have air raid shelters per se in our village, but whenever there was an air raid (American by day, British by night), my parents, or my mother, if my father was at work, and I would burrow into the hay and straw in our barn, closing our eyes tightly and holding our hands over our ears. There really was no place to run. In the event, I never saw a bombed house or the actual wreckage of a plane. But my dreams were full of them. We worried a great deal about my father, because of his being out along the railway lines, which were major targets for the Allied planes.

Even by a child's accounting, there was increasing scarcity of almost everything. Food, of course, was first and foremost, even well before the Hunger Winter. Clothing of all kinds, but especially shoes, and even the leather to repair them. Warmth, and it was not uncommon to not know whether you were colder when you were in the house, or outside it. It became almost impossible to find replacement tires for our bicycles, which were our only form of transport besides our poorly-shod feet. The Hunger Winter, when it arrived in late 1944, was really just a very harsh extension of privation, and not a new calamity.

The only things I had a surfeit of during those five years were uncertainty, fear, and sorrow. Now that I am an adult at 18, I sometimes am thankful that I experienced the Occupation as a child, and not as an adult, for the adults better understood the terrors behind the terrors, and the possibilities and expectations of ever-greater cruelty and misfortune. But then again I sometimes think of how bewildering it was, being a child, and not understanding as fully the detailed hows and whys behind those experiences of fear and sorrow.

But, after the landings in France, and the miracle of the Liberation of Paris in August of 1944, we did know the Allies were coming. The Americans, British, and Canadians were coming to save us, coming to drive the Germans away. And, as summer was ending in 1944, and we were getting ready for school, we hoped it would be soon. We talked of having all the food you wanted to eat, of having warm clothes for the winter to come, even of having new toys again--- all these things which were only half-remembered.

As the Allied forces moved up into Belgium and even into the southern part of our country, we dared to believe it would be soon. Even the Germans believed it would be soon, for they became somewhat less aggressive to us in the street, and began to spend more time clustered together in their barracks.

And then Queen Wilhelmina, from England, sent a message to us, received via hundreds of clandestine radio sets, and multiplied a thousand times by illicit leaflets and wall-pasted posters, and then multiplied again a million times by voices, mostly in whispers but in occasional shouts: "Get Ready. The Liberation is coming. Soon. The Liberation is coming soon!"

On that day in September, known since then as 'Mad Tuesday', people poured into the streets, shouting, laughing, dancing, hugging. Dancing in the streets, while the Germans stayed in their barracks. No child was in school that day. Bottles of long-hoarded schnapps were poured out liberally to friends and complete strangers alike.

And the Queen especially asked that the Railroad Workers go on a wildcat strike. Prevent the Germans from moving men and materials at will. Sabotage the railroads. Cripple the enemies of our country. Rise up and liberate the Netherlands!

And the Railroad workers, Jacob Vermeer among them, were ready. Many more than 2 or 3 came to the house that night, and lit lanterns, and agreed that It Was Time. And the same meeting was held in a thousand other small houses, all across the northern Netherlands. And the next day the trains did not run.

But the next day the Allies did not come. Nor did they come the day after. Nor the day after that.

For their planned attack at Arnhem, which was designed to then advance north completely through the Netherlands, failed, and the Germans stopped them, for a time, at the River Wall.

The Allies then turned east, not north, crossing the Rhine, heading directly into Germany, aimed at Berlin.

The Germans in the Netherlands must have known that their defeat was only a matter of time, that they had no way to go in any direction but backwards. But they were furious, and perhaps felt shamed, especially by the railway strike.

They brought in German railway workers, but not enough to break the strike. So, in vengeance, they announced a complete boycott of food, fuel, and other essentials into Northern and Eastern Holland, all of which would have had to travel by rail. They also detonated explosives to destroy many dikes, making travel and transport even more difficult, and, more importantly, flooding farmland, killing any still-standing crops and making the next Spring planting impossible. It was a deliberately cruel punishment, without significant strategic military value. It was done to make us suffer.

Certainly, as a child of 12, I would have not understood all these considerations and their detailed implications. But I understood the fear on my parents' faces, their hushed conversations, and I understood two sentences: Where will the food come from? What will become of us?

We were used to privation. By this time in 1944, our milk cow was long gone, confiscated by the Germans. Pigs were a distant memory. We had one goat left, and a few chickens, none of whom seemed to be laying eggs any longer. Our cat, Pumpkin, had disappeared, probably gone feral. Our dog Highball was still with us, but as it turned out, only for a few months more: then he also disappeared, probably stolen and eaten as the famine worsened.

I did not know it, of course, but my mother had missed two menstrual periods, and was pregnant. She, my father, and I sat around the kitchen table as, with tears in his eyes, he held my hand and said the worst words I have ever heard.

"Christina, I am going to have to 'dive'. The Germans will come looking for me now, and they must not find me. I cannot tell you or your mother where I am going, or with whom, lest the Germans make you tell them. I must go tonight, and I will try to get word to you as soon as I can that I am safe and well. Of course I will come back to you as soon as I can. You must be your mother's best helper while I am gone. I know you are strong, and I love you very much. "

I knew what the word 'dive' meant. It was Dutch Resistance slang for going into hiding, or of being hidden by others. To me it had always connoted diving down into cold black water, deep, deep water, water with no bottom. And no way back up into the light of day.

And so my father left us that night. He took his warmest jacket, threadbare that it was, his black wool stocking cap, a few things thrown into his railway work bag, and that was about all. There was a soft knock on the kitchen window, Father blew out the kerosene lamp on the wooden dining table, hugged my Mother and myself, opened the door, and stepped out into the blackness.

Of course, I never saw him again. And the Hunger Winter came upon us as we were.

My mother and I knew we were strong-willed. We were determined to survive and to keep our house for Father to return to. I was a skinny beanpole of a girl, straight hips, tiny breast buds, years from my first monthly. Like all the children of the Occupation, I was an expert in deception. Mother told me about her pregnancy, and how it might complicate things as the months moved along. We knew that the first and most important problem would be food, but I don't think, looking back now, that either of us realized that this would be a struggle for survival, and not just a struggle to overcome want and privation.

October and early November were, in retrospect, not that much worse than what we had already experienced: we still had the remnants of our own resources, and there were still some supplies in the food shops, though they dwindled rapidly. We scrounged wood for warmth and cooking, first using up our small "winter woodpile" and then finding what we could of branches and small logs in the nearby fields and woods. Some food supplies came in illicitly, mostly by small skiffs along the many canals. Prices for everything rose, of course, but the black-marketing was not as bad as it could have been. After four years of German Occupation, everyone except the major collaborators was poor, and without significant savings, so, especially in the small towns and villages, there was only so much increase that the shop-owners could ask. Most of us, Hardy Dutch that we were, believed that we would face a difficult time, and surmount it.

And then, in November, the canals froze over. The illicit boat trafficking ended. It became clear that an unusually cold and long winter lay ahead.

As the cold and hunger increased, people shut themselves up in their houses, put on all the clothes that they could find, and looked for wood to burn. In the cities, I heard, the wooden ties of the trolley tracks were torn up by people searching for fuel. As the winter wore on, we, like everyone else, began to burn what we could of our

barn, and then our own house around us—first the stairway bannis-
ter, then some cupboard doors, then any chair we did not need to sit
on, or any drawer we did not need to close. My mother and I slept
close together, but in my bed, which was smaller and thus conserved
more heat.

Thus we fought the Winter. But by Christmas we had to also
fight the Hunger—the real Hunger, the Starvation Hunger, the
Hunger which did not only punish, but the Hunger which killed.

The allowable food rations set by the Dutch Government
(actually, by the Germans) became tighter and tighter. By January,
an adult was authorized 2 slices of bread, 2 small potatoes, and a half
of a sugar beet per day. No additional protein, no fats, no oils, no
vitamins, nothing else. This was, of course, not enough to live on; it
was only enough to schedule a path to dying on.

The infants, even those who were breast-fed, died first. Then
the old people, especially the men, and those who were invalids and
could not fight the daily fight that it took to keep back the cold and
the starvation.

I did not know my grandparents on my father's side. Apparently
there had been some family quarrel when he and my mother married, severe enough to cause a permanent rupture.

But my mother's parents, who still lived in Amersfoort, I did
know, though we did not see them very often. In late February, my
grandfather contracted pneumonia, and that and the Hunger carried
him off. My mother asked my surviving grandmother, who was herself of course starving, to come and live with us. She refused, saying
that an extra mouth, especially given my mother's pregnancy, might
tip the scales against us all, and that she would stay in her Amersfoort
cottage and find a way through until the Germans were gone.

Then my mother told me the story that she and my father had never told me. My mother's grandmother (my grandmother's mother on my mother's side) had been a Jew, born in Amsterdam, who converted to Christianity when she married my great-grandfather and moved with him to Amersfoort. Perhaps this marriage had been the cause of the rupture between my father and his parents when he married my mother, who was the granddaughter of a Jew, but my mother was not sure about this.

What she was sure of, however, was that this this was the reason why we never saw much of my mother's parents after the Nazi Occupation began. My grandmother was afraid that her Jewish ancestry would be discovered, especially if anyone looked up the old records if they moved residence, and that our entire family, down to me, might be persecuted and sent to the extermination camps. Such was life in the Netherlands during the Occupation. My mother added that she was certain that my grandfather's death was hastened by his giving the larger share of his daily food ration to his wife.

Yes, the Hunger Winter was long, and it was cold. Many, perhaps 20,000, Dutch died of starvation. Many others, like my grandfather, died "of" something else, such as pneumonia, but might have lived had there not been the starvation beneath it.

But many of us, like my mother and I, survived. We survived, above all, because of four interlinked factors:

1. The bicycle.

2. The courage of Dutch women, who rode most of the bicycles.

3. The fact that the Hunger Winter, though long and cold, contained little or no snow, so that the bicycles could be ridden on roads and rural paths and across fields.

4. The Food Airlift by the British and Americans, which came very late, but just in time to save us.

I am not clear as to just how the idea of using one's bicycle to gather food from the countryside began. It seems it was spontaneous, and natural, given the ubiquitous cycling of the Dutch in our small, relatively flat, nation. Men, women, children all rode bikes to work, to school, to shop, to visit, and also just for pleasure. Now they had to ride bicycles to keep themselves and their families from starving.

By January of 1945, we were, all of us, desperate for food. People were digging up and roasting tulip bulbs to eat, from their own gardens or, increasingly, from the commercial tulip fields. And, as it became clear that, if there was no food anywhere else, there must be some food available on the rural farmlands, whether the left-over gleanings, or harvested crops which could not be transported because of the German boycott. It also became clear that bicycles could take people to that food, and carry significant loads of it back home

So, in ever-increasing numbers, people began to take their bicycles in what became called 'Going to the Farms', to buy, beg, borrow, or steal things that they could eat to keep themselves and their families alive.

Many of those who went 'To the Farms' were men or boys, but this was extremely dangerous. Males were more likely to be stopped by German patrols, with high chance of arrest and deportation to slave labor or worse. Women were much less likely to be harassed or arrested. Best of all for this task were young adolescents, and girls better than boys.

By January, we had had no word at all of my father's whereabouts, his condition, or whether he was alive or not. Had he been arrested, shot, enslaved, deported, ill, injured, or was he (unlikely) safe and healthy? Would we never hear from him again, or would he, one night, walk into our kitchen looking as he looked when he had left it? My mother and I shifted from anxiety to hope and to despair, round and round. By late January we faced up to reality and agreed to stop discussing it. What would be would be. This was, for me, the beginning of 'The End of Dreams', and the capstone of the end of my childhood.

What it was for my mother, I am not sure, but she became increasingly uncommunicative; we could work together all day long, undertaking the mundane tasks of staying alive, and hardly exchange a word beyond those absolutely essential. Part of this was the fatigue and depression of starvation; part of it was something else, perhaps the focused all-encompassing determination for survival.

Both of us shed flesh from our bones. Her pregnancy seemed to proceed normally, albeit a ghastly cartoon of a stick and bones and skull-faced figure with a protuberant belly.

And so, at age twelve, in mid-winter, I became the food-gatherer and 'bread-winner' for what remained of our family.

By the time of the Hunger Winter, many, if not most, of the millions of bicycles in the Netherlands had badly-worn tires, if indeed they had tires at all. Tires of all kinds had been requisitioned and confiscated by the Germans, and replacements were contraband items. Private automobiles and trucks had virtually disappeared from the roads, horses and wagons became fewer (as the horses were eaten), and the boat canals were frozen over. So the bicycle was the crucial form of non-foot transport.

My father was a very careful and farsighted man. He also, because of his work, would know when a few bicycle tires might be found to 'fall off' a railroad car headed for Germany. So, hidden in our small barn, deep in the hay, were six or more serviceable (but not new, that would have been suspicious) tires for our three bicycles, which had stood, tire-less and seemingly innocent, by the barn door. Thus, we were more fortunate than many of the others who had to 'Go To The Farms' with bare or badly-patched tires, or thick hemp rope wound around the wheel rims, or, worst of all, travel on the bare rims themselves (yes, some actually did, in great discomfort and significant danger).

I must admit that, though it was difficult, and in some sense dangerous, I loved 'Going To The Farms'. In place of grinding poverty, hunger, and terror, it was freedom, wind in the face, adventure, challenge. The winter landscape was open, clear, and virtually empty of other travelers (except for others on the same missions, who became co-conspirators). We were doing something actively for ourselves and our loved ones, and actively AGAINST the Germans. We had to be clever, strong, daring, ingenious, positive—all the things we were not allowed to be during the Occupation. Our lives depended upon our own actions, not on the whims and orders and cruelty of those who had dominated us for so long. Yes, I loved it; the only thing which would have made it more perfect would have been if Highball could have been there to run alongside me. But, alas, he was gone, as was so much else.

I carried with me a couple of burlap sacks (which cushioned my seat when empty, and which hung from the handlebars when full), a bit of twine, some few notes and coins from our nearly-empty jar in the kitchen, whatever small objects might be desired by others in trade for food (buttons, a spool or two of thread and some needles, ornaments, old gloves, and so forth), and two tools: a small sharp knife (for anything overlooked or left behind on a tree or stalk) and a small hand-trowel (for digging up anything left in the earth that could be eaten).

What I am about to tell you now, I have never before told a soul, not even my mother: one of my schoolteachers asked me if I would carry leaflets to distribute in the countryside, or post up however I thought best and safest, leaflets urging the Dutch to stand fast and resist, that Liberation and freedom were coming. Of course I did this, and imagined I could see my father's face on every copy. The more of this I did, the less I was afraid.

There were many ways to gather food from the farms. The easiest, but the least productive as time went on, was to glean from the empty fields: digging up the missed potato or turnip, finding the forgotten stalk of corn, capturing the dropped squash or pumpkin. The same went for whatever apple might still be hanging on the treetop. There were also all sorts of roots that could be dug up for cooking and eating, such as the famous tulip bulbs. All these things could be gathered with, or without, the knowledge and agreement of the farmer. The latter method, if necessary, is stealing. So be it. Stealing is better than starving.

Or, one could approach the farm family directly, and beg for some of their crop. Some would actually respond positively to this. Not many, but some. I have even had, more than once, a farmer and his wife offer me dinner, a night's sound sleep, breakfast, and some food to take home with me. They were usually, but not always by any means, an elderly childless couple, and I bless them all to this day.

Begging is better than stealing, but in my experience usually less effective.

Or, one could offer to trade, or to pay money, in exchange for food. This is probably the most effective method.

Do not let me appear to be cynical about this. If it were not for the caring and generosity of the Dutch farm families during the Hunger Winter, the number of deaths would have been much higher than it was.

So, from January through April, I 'Went to the Farms'. I loved the travel and the countryside. I learned much about people, and much about myself. Depending on how much food I came back with, and whatever else my mother could find at home, I would generally go about once a week. Usually it was out and back the same day. If I could not find a farmer who would let me sleep in his barn, or in his house, I had to be very careful, and judge time and distance correctly, and not get caught out to have to spend a night out in the fields. It was bitter cold, killing cold, and my burlap bags would not have been enough to survive by. This was really my only fear, of freezing to death. I saw no Germans, except for an occasional patrol near the towns, I had no fear of my fellow seekers (in fact, we would sometimes collaborate in various ways), there were no wild animals, and crime (except for stealing food) was virtually unknown.

This was all, I fear, difficult for my mother, who needed to send me, but did not know when I would be back, as there was no way to send a message from a farmhouse. It was only years later that I realized that every time I was away 'Going To The Farms', she would have to think about my father's unknown journey.

So we survived, though it was difficult, and painful, and exhausting, and depressing. As Winter and early Spring came in their turn, the routines required for survival became, as they do, routine. Everyone we knew was skeletal. Every edge, every inch had to be finely calculated. Sickness and death of friends and neighbors lost their power to shock, but not their power to wound.

I think, in a strange way, that had we not had the Germans to hate, and to fear, and to blame, more of us would have given in, and just faded away. But we had them, and they had us, and we would not give in.

Near the end of March, we almost lost our will. We had no word nor sign from my father. My mother's time arrived; our neighbor came to assist the birth. My mother was beyond gaunt and grey, but labor progressed normally and relatively easily, and my baby brother was born, fully developed and alive, though very small. My mother's milk came in quickly, and the baby, as yet without a name, sucked hungrily. Before the week was out, he was dead.

How we survived after that, I really could not say. Perhaps it was by finding, not the need to take, but the need to give. Another neighbor, whose husband had been arrested by the Germans a few months earlier, delivered her own baby a week after my brother was born. She was so malnourished that her milk supply was not nearly adequate. So my mother, whose breasts were not yet dried up, went to her neighbor's house, four times a day, and suckled her friend's child, who has survived and thrived these 5 years. My mother says that this was her greatest joy, and her greatest sadness, apart from my father and his disappearance.

So there we were, on the knife's edge, not knowing whether or not we had the sustenance, nor the strength, nor at the end, the will, to carry on.

And then the Allies came to save us. Not on the ground, not at first, but from the sky. The airplanes of the British and the Americans came, to drop food from the air, so close as to almost touch the yet-to-sprout Spring grass, and delivered us from the Hunger Winter.

The German Army surrendered the Netherlands on May 5, and the war ended formally on May 8, 1945. We were free again, though faced with the problems of defining and experiencing normal lives in a world, which, to me, was nothing like anything I had experienced previously. I thought often about my father's final words to me, eons ago and less than a year previously. I realized that I was also a 'diver', but one who now had to come up for air and rediscover who she was and what world she lived in.

And that was the end of my Third Life, and the beginning of my Fourth, which has yet to take its final shape.

JACOB RILEY, SR. (1950)

Since I got home from my war in Europe, people who had known me before, as a kid of 19, say that I am much changed. That I am remote, and wary, and slow to laughter, and seeming sometimes to be elsewhere rather than where I am. Not eager and bushy-tailed and open, as I was before.

This is probably so, and I did not get home to Topeka from my war until early 1946, given the hospital and recovery time, first at Base Hospital in England, then at the Veterans Hospital in Missouri. Despite my chest and arm and neck burn scars, and my short right leg, and the nightmares, I thought I actually was a pretty lucky Joe, compared to many. I was alive, my parents were as well, my girl Betsey had waited for me (we were married two weeks after I got home), and so I was much better off than a lot of guys, especially my B-17 crew buddies, of whom I was the only one who came back from our thirtieth mission. More about that later.

And I had also lost my kid brother, Ernie, who enlisted with the Marines at age 19, in 1943, and was killed going over the wall as a rifleman before he reached 20, in a place called Red Beach Three on some island named Tarawa. I missed Ernie, still miss him and always will, but I think my folks had made the right decision over those long three years when I was in my own Hell in Europe. They didn't tell me that Ernie was gone until I myself was safely home.

So, yes, I have changed. Who could not have? Airplanes had been my heart's desire and delight since I was 15. Now I have promised myself I will never fly again, not even as a passenger. I keep to myself and my family (to Betsey, and to my son, Jake, and my parents, Matthew and Edna) pretty much, but I am not quarrelsome nor offensive, and I stay out of trouble. I guess I am lucky that my Dad has been so successful in his business ventures here in Topeka, so that there is a secure place here for me (and my skills; I can pull my own weight). I'm not sure I have, at least not yet, the initiative or spark to break new trails. Quiet is good.

A good deal of my inner life is spent in considering one set of questions, which have to do with what happened, on our 30th mission, to my plane the "Big Chief" (I was the co-pilot on the B-17). Less than two weeks before the war finally ended, we went down, and I was the only one who got out. So I ask myself, "Why me and not them?" Or, "Why not me and why them?" I wonder if I should have stayed with them, not fought my way out of the ship after she went down, stayed with them. Was it right for me to be here, and them to be wherever they were?

Well, as someone once said, "It is necessary to begin at the beginning", so here goes:

I suppose I had the All-American boyhood, growing up in the 1920's and 1930's. My Mom and Dad were the real thing, self-made pioneer types, both of whom were born poor and then struck oil on their Land Rush homestead in Oklahoma, and moved to Topeka, Kansas. My Dad, Matthew Riley, got in early on opportunity, as he always seemed to be able to do, owning the Ford Motor Agency in town, and then seizing the next opportunity to make, buy, and sell parts and equipment for the aircraft industry that was making Topeka call itself "The Airline Capitol of The World." The Great Depression didn't hit Topeka, or the Rileys, too hard, because the stockyards were still full of beef, the railroad still shipped it in and out, the farmers still grew grain (the Great Dust Bowl was mainly west of us) and, if they bought fewer new tractors and motor vehicles, they still bought them from us, and the aircraft industry was still booming. So, in my childhood I never knew want.

I was a better ball player than a student in school, but I did OK. When I was 15 years old and a freshman in High School, Dad took me to a barnstorming Air Show: barrel rolls and wing-walkers and all, and that was it, True Love, for me. Dad asked a friend who flew crop dusters to take me up for a ride. It was in an old World War I-vintage bi-plane, and from that moment on my future was in the skies.

I started college at Kansas State in Manhattan, planning to major in Engineering, but was, to tell the truth, more bored than inspired. When the US got into the War in 1941, I saw my main chance, like my father had, and took it. I dropped out of school, joined the Army, got into the Army Air Corps (there was no separate Air Force back then) and applied for Flight School.

I did all right, not brilliant but pretty good, earned my Commission as Second Lieutenant, and qualified on the B-17 Boeing Flying Fortress as Co-Pilot. In early 1943 I finally realized that this was serious business, when we flew over to England to a US airbase just built for us in the Midlands. We were going to bomb the hell out of Hitler, that is what we said. Just before we left the US, I had a short furlough home, and I asked my High School Sweetheart, Betsey Rourke, to "wait for me." She said she would. What with flying a

B-17, and Betsey, I thought I was pretty much Jack Armstrong, "The All-American Boy" as the radio and comic books had it, just like a million other guys thought they were.

Being in England was ok, because we weren't really in Lakenheath, England: we were on a United States Army Air Base. We all knew our jobs, and were very serious about them, and if I may say so, very good at them, even if our job was flying twenty-something thousand feet above the earth, usually in the daylight, blowing things up and killing people who, mostly, we never saw. The ones we actually saw were in other airplanes, trying to kill us, so there was a certain feeling of unreality about it all.

Our anchors to the realities, both physical and emotional, were two things: our ship, and our crew. You would give anything you had for and to either. And you expected the same in return. Home was very far away. We knew what we were fighting for, but, as I said, it was very far away. We waited between missions mostly for the next mission, reliving the action, and the terror, and the rush, and the hope, and the dread, and the relief, of the last one, and counting off the numbers. Flyers live by numbers: altitude, speed, compass direction, distance, time. And combat flyers add: bomb weight and release coordinates, time to and over target, numbers of our ships lost on the mission, numbers of enemy attackers shot down (and by whom), time back to safe base, fuel needed to make it.

In 1943 and 44, only one B-17 crew member in four survived to reach his 25th (and later 30th) mission and complete his combat tour. So, no matter how all the numbers added up, we all knew that they were not in our favor.

What an airplane that was! Our ship was the new model B-17 F, with the new 50 caliber machine guns (replacing the old 30 cals) poking out from fore and aft, bottom, top, and port and starboard sides. She could fly for nearly ten hours, reaching max speeds of almost two hundred miles per, cruise and bomb from ten to twenty-nine thousand feet altitude, and deliver four thousand pounds of bombs.

Yes, indeed, she was a Flying Fortress, with a crew of ten brass-balled young Americans, living for the moment, and by the hour. Putting on a brave face and a cocky manner, but basically scared shitless most all of the time.

There were problems with the B-17, however. She was unheated and unpressurized. These meant there were hours of bitter cold, with temperatures that could reach sixty degrees below zero, and the cold thin air at high altitude required oxygen masks with tank connection, and thick oversuits with plug in to heating wiring. Parachutes were too bulky to wear routinely, but you had them close by on a hook-on line. When you were under attack, by German fighter planes or anti-aircraft flak, you were supposed to wear an armored vest and a helmet. Guess how many of us did.

The B-17's job in Europe was to engage in massive bombing raids in daylight, flying in 'Big Box' stacked formations, to take advantage of the planes' all-direction defensive fire-power. Up to a thousand ships would form a heavy raid, and you were to take off, be directed into your place in formation, and stay in formation, no matter what, until you dropped your load, then break and run for the coast, the English Channel, and home base. These raids were mostly over the railroads and heavy industry in Germany. My buddies and I arrived in time to take part in the heavy 1943 raids on Bremen and Schweinfurt, and what a hell of a baptism of fire that was.

Until we got the longer-distance fighter planes that could help defend us against the attacking German fighters during much of our flight, we took extremely heavy losses in men and aircraft. The German fighters were good pilots in great machines, and though the B-17 all-directional armament was effective, it was by itself inadequate. Later in 1944, when we got the P-47 and P-51 fast longer-range fighters, God Bless Them, things got much better for us. But, even still, until the required 25 missions to complete a tour (raised to 30 in 1944) and until we received that improved fighter support, only one out of four US B-17 crewmen survived to complete their tour. That's right, as I said twice before, and it was and still is always on my mind, only one out of four.

The anti-aircraft flak was our other hazard (not counting 'minor' troubles like bad weather or instrument or mechanical failure). You would be sitting up there looking down at those beautiful multi-colored blooms, wondering when the one that you didn't see was going to blow you away.

All in all, life for us Yankee fliers was, like the man said, "Nasty, brutish, and short."

So we loved our airplane, and maybe the only time we felt 'safe' was actually when it was most dangerous, when our ten-man crew was together inside her skin, linked together by radio and oxygen lines, and sense of mission, and support for one another. Sounds crazy, I know, but it had a certain logic to it.

Ten of us. Not forever the same ten, of course. We lost four guys in our first six months of missions, and I can hardly remember all their names, though I remember their positions: two waist gunners, one ball-turret gunner, and one bombardier. The waist gunners were shot to death by an attacking German fighter, the ball-turret gunner the same. The bombardier, after he had dropped his load on target, fell out of his little space below the plane's nose, when a fighter shot it to pieces. We never knew whether he had been shot dead, or whether he had dropped out of the tattered plexi-glass alive. On that mission, we limped safely home with a mangled nose and the port-side wing ditto alongside the fuselage. The B-17 had a reputation for being extremely rugged and able to make it home, as the song went, "On a Wing and a Prayer", and that day we surely did, with as much prayer as wing, and our pilot's skill.

After that, we seemed to lead a charmed life, and we lost only one other guy, the rear turret tail gunner, Tiny, until that very last mission, the Thirtieth, when we lost them all, or lost them all except me, and I returned to tell the tale, and to dream about it, I am sure, for the rest of my life.

We lost Tiny on Mission number 24. We called him Tiny, not because, as usual G.I slang would have it, he was very big, but because he really was very small, tiny really, skinny, and just up to regulation minimum height. But he could move like a spider, and react twice as fast, and shoot very straight, in Tiny's tiny bubble at the far tail of the ship, the most important defensive position, where the German fighters' liked best to attack. Tiny saved our bacon many times. On the day we lost him, a German beat him to the punch, shot up the turret. Tiny screamed over the radio that he was hit bad and bleeding worse. As I was the co-pilot whose job it was most often to react to casualties in the crew, I grabbed the med kit and worked my way back to the tail. Tiny was curled on the deck, blood coming out of his mouth and spurting like a fountain from his neck, where an artery must have taken a hit. With the turret shot away it was as cold as Hell Frozen Over. As I grabbed him and tried to apply pressure to the left side of his neck, I could sense the flow lessen and then stop altogether. He died as I held him, not a word said.

Our pilot, Les Dalton, was one hell of a great one. He had been an Army Air Corps pilot even before the War started. You would imagine he could fly a frying pan, and he knew every trick and every toggle of the B-17. We called him "More" (because Less is More), he was the Captain, every inch of him. Of course I was, as the Co-Pilot, (called "Jerk" or even "Jerk-Off" instead of Jacob), and was more than a little jealous of More, but I knew he was not only the top dog, but the best one. He was my hero, and all of two years older than I was.

More was from Montana, and I, of course, was from Kansas. Especially because of my Mom's claim that she was one-quarter Cherokee, and because of us two guys in the front seats being from the Great West, as the others would have it, there was a lot of back and forth about Cowboys and Indians, and as I will tell you in a minute, that led to the name we chose for our plane.

The Flight Engineer (who also served as the top turret gunner to protect against fighter planes diving on us from above) was the general fix-it guy who knew what all the systems were and how to repair them in flight, hopefully). This was Byron James, 'Bye', and, like my father, he seemed to be able to fix anything, out of any materials. Maybe hold the 'Big Chief' together with piano wire and paper clips.

Our Navigator, Will Stanton, we called 'Maps.' He was from Pennsylvania, and wore glasses when he could get away with it, and had been planning to become a math teacher before the War started. He had, when we were on the ground, a bad stutter, but when he was doing his job in-flight, he spoke clear as a bell.

Radio Operator, Rudy Collins, from Ohio, was of course 'Sparks'. He had a wicked and very obscene sense of humor, and, when we were not terrified, was responsible for keeping us laughing.

Bombardier, Ryan West, was from California, and it took him a little while to fit in after his predecessor fell out of the airplane (we never told him those details), and was for a while kind of the odd man out of the crew. Very quiet, kept to himself a good deal on base. The bombardier had probably the toughest job of the crew, except for the pilot, given the technical requirements of dropping the load just at the right time and in the right place. By 1944 he got a big boost with the top-secret installation of what was called only the 'Blue Ox', a new type of 'computer' (whatever that means) bombsight that somehow ran the necessary calculations. In fact, as the plane came on final approach for the delivery, precise control of the aircraft was actually transferred from the pilot to the bombardier for the critical minutes preceding the drop.

The bombardier also served as the gunner in the nose turret, when he was not actually engaged in dropping high explosives to blow up things and kill people far below.

The port and starboard Waist Gunners, Bob Gross, our second Ohioan, and Billybob Dillon, from Mississippi, we called the Bobsey Twins, after the popular children's book series. I never could quite keep straight which was at the port and which was at the starboard position.

The Ball Turret gunner was under the fuselage, and could shoot down around the clock. Our guy was another Rudy, Rudy Turel, from New Hampshire, so we called him 'Rudy Two' or more likely Rudy Toot, to distinguish him from Rudy Collins, the Radio Operator.

And that, along with the all-important Tail Gunner, was us. After we lost Tiny, another guy, named George Wilson, from Kansas, like me, was transferred to us; he had been tail gunner on another B-17 that had made it back from over Germany with only George, and the pilot, and two other guys, alive. The survivors were broken up as a team, and George came to us. That was difficult, given the circumstances of our losses and his. He was a fine guy, and a good gunner. But he never really fit in, more our fault than his. He never had a nick-name.

We were together, through the flak and the weather, all the way through to that Thirtieth mission, when they, all except me, bought the farm. And while I didn't kill them, I sure as Hell didn't save any of them, and that will always be with me.

Every crew, following the pilot's lead, named their airplane. Names varied, from the aggressive, to the truly humorous. But our ship was not only our home and refuge, it (or She, almost universally) was our identity, the connection that bound us together, in the most terrible or even in the most beautiful of circumstances.

So, she needed to have a name, and the name had to somehow tell us, and our enemies, and the world, who we were.

After much discussion, some of it not printable, Tiny proposed that, since we were on the Warpath, and since the two front-seaters were closely related to John Wayne and Geronimo, she be named "The Big Chief". This met with general approval, especially after More produced an amateur artist from among the Squadron's Ground Crew, who in turn produced the following character, to be painted, life-sized, on the left front of the fuselage.

Big Chief she was, but with strong resemblance to movie-star Betty Grable, especially in the length of her smooth and very shapely legs, one stretched out forward, one bent at the knee. Both feet were bare, and flexed forward with toes pointed. She was sitting, but not upright, rather she leaned back sinuously on two palms stretched to the ground behind her. Her ample (actually, more than ample) chest also angled up, out, and back, and pushed against a tight (very tight) vest, complementing her short (very short) shorts. Her head was also tipped back, and atop her long hair was a complete feathered War Bonnet, and it had a long feathered tail.

Wow! The Big Chief! Holy Kimoley! Shazzam!

We were young, and randy, but mostly inexperienced in anything but killing. There were pubs in the countryside around the base, and we would go and drink their warm and terrible beer when we could. Sometimes we would mix with the Brits from other bases, but mostly the two groups kept to themselves. There was seldom trouble, and seldom close interaction, between us and them. I know the Brits had a saying about the Yanks being "Overpaid, Oversexed, and Over Here" but this was more half in jest than anything else. I had great respect for the Brits, their grit and the pounding they had taken. Their bomber pilots and crews were resolute; the spirit and unconquerable courage of their Spitfire fighter pilots became legendary. Mr. Churchill said, "Never have so many owed so much to so few." I always thought that by "so many" he must have meant the whole world.

The Brits, in their heavy Lancaster Bombers, flew the night-time raids. We, in our B-17s, flew the daytime. It was a source of endless argument as to who had the most dangerous assignment, and who had the 'easy ride.' So we kept pounding Germany, day and night. But a lot of our planes fell out of the sky.

One time More and Tiny and I got a three-day pass and went in to see London, or what was left of it. We picked up some girls, went drinking, and then to a cheap hotel. Nothing very serious happened; there were six of us and only two beds. Just a lot of fooling and fiddling around, and a bit of needed temporary amnesia for all concerned.

I should say a word about the music, speaking of being young. I had always loved music, especially growing up in the radio and movie days of the late Twenties and Thirties. My brother Ernie played a medium good guitar, and we used to sing along together.

Early in the War, 1941, before I even got overseas, the Andrews Sisters (who were the Best of the Best for us young guys) had the first big 'military' hit: "The Boogie-Woogie Bugle Boy of Company B", which was all really about the draft, and kids leaving home to serve their country.

Then, in 1942, as the reality of so many going away, for an unknown time, to unknown places, and maybe not coming back, the Andrews Sisters were singing: "Don't Sit Under the Apple Tree". Of course, it always made me think of Betsey.

And then, in 1943, just as I was really getting into it, came the biggest war hit of all, sung first by the Song Spinners: "Coming in on a Wing and a Prayer":

That one was very close to us; we had seen it, and we had done it. And we had seen lots of guys who hadn't made it. Sometimes, on the way 'home' after a mission, we would all sing it to each other over the intercom. But only after we had crossed the Channel, and could almost see our base up close.

For those of us who were flying, this was really our song. And I guess it was America's as well, because it was a tremendous hit. Everybody recorded it: Sammy Kaye, Glen Miller, even Frank Sinatra and, you guessed it, the Andrews Sisters.

While I was in England, I heard the songs of Vera Lynn: "White Cliffs of Dover", and "We'll Meet Again." You could tell immediately the difference between the sad longing of the Brits, who had had such a dreadful time of it, personally and as a nation, and endured it with such courage, and the uppity persistence among the Americans of what, after the First World War, was called that "Yankee Doodledy Dum."

"We'll meet again"... we all knew what that meant. It didn't matter if you were American or English, you knew what that song was about, and that Special Someone who, hopefully, was still singing it for you. For when, and if, you made it back.

But of course it wasn't a cake walk for us, either. Each mission was a terrifying encounter with the unknown. We saw B-17's just drop out of the Big Box, either exploding, or losing parts along the way, or just dropping. Sometimes parachutes would flare, we always looked for them, but sometimes the planes just went down. Sometimes the anti-aircraft flak would get a direct hit on a plane near us in the formation, and debris, which we knew included bits of our buddies, would spatter in all directions. Sometimes we would watch a wounded aircraft turn and limp for far-off home base, only to curve into altitude loss and, far away, disintegrate into the ground. And sometimes a German fighter, or several, would target onto a wounded airplane already trailing smoke, and shoot it into pieces like wolves on a crippled deer.

When those German fighter aircraft came at us, from one or several directions at once, and their machine gun rounds came clanging onto, or through, the 'Big Chief', we hated those bastards, and wanted to kill them, shoot them to pieces, and when we did, we cheered and howled like those wolves. And, I suppose, they did the same with us.

About the bombing, it was more complicated. At first, I thought about what was happening down there as a result of our actions. The people, most all civilians—men, women, children, and dogs and cats-- we were killing. Then after a while, I said to myself I was just doing my job, and it was a job that had to be done for my country, and so I better stop thinking about it and just do it as well as I could. And that's what I did. But I never cheered when I saw the explosions come up.

Of course, as Co-Pilot, I never pulled a trigger, so to speak. But I knew I was lying if I ever thought I was just along for the ride. I was there to help kill people and smash things; that's the way it was.

But sometimes you'd owe a guy from another crew a beer, or had a harsh word with someone, or been asked a question that you hadn't answered. And then you go up in the Big Box, and his plane would not come back, though yours did. What then?

So that's how it was for me and my buddies on the Big Chief. By mid-April, 1945, we knew the Germans were on their last legs, despite their final winter surge at the Battle of the Bulge. And our crew, charmed as our lives had been since we lost Tiny, which seemed so long ago, were coming up on Mission 28—when the Word came down.

All heavy bomber raids would end as of April 27.

It was difficult for us to take it all in. If we just survived three more missions, or if April 27 came first, we would come off the line and into some maybe-cushy ground or staff position. No more flak, no more German fighter attacks. No more worrying if you had enough fuel, Wing, or Prayer to make it back to base. Maybe you would even be going back Stateside, almost inconceivable. And a little bit ambivalent, just a little. Because with the dread and terror of every mission also came the rush and the thrill.

The Big Chief did not fly another bombing mission. We were so relieved, but also so lost. Our purpose, terrible as it had been, was no longer ours. And how about those guys, whoever they were, who would fly before April 27, and some of them not come back?

And then the Second Word came down, just behind the ever-present rumors on April 25.

It had been decided, "At the Highest Level", that we and the Brits would fly rescue missions, "Missions of Mercy", over the Netherlands, and drop food supplies to the starving Dutch. We knew the Germans were still there, we had been still dodging their flak until now. But apparently a deal had been worked out where the Germans would not shoot at us, and we would not bomb them, as we swooped in and dropped our loads of food. Special areas would be marked out on the ground, special times for the drops agreed, and everybody concerned would hold fire. The Brits were to begin on April 29, we would start on May 1. The Operation (called by the Brits "Operation Manna", and by us "Operation Chowhound"), would last about ten days.

On April 27, we had our first briefing on Chowhound. Food pallets would be dropped without parachutes. We would come in to the drop site at only 400 feet altitude, drop our loads, and get the Hell out of there and back home.

We were thunder-struck. How could we know that it wasn't a trick, that the Germans wouldn't pot shoot us at point-blank range? How could we know the drop-sites would be correctly marked? And most of all, how could heavy bombers fly through and drop the load at only 400 feet above the ground?

Will (Maps) Stanton, the Navigator and math whiz, put on his glasses. He thought for an instant, and then said, without a trace of a stammer, "This is crazy. Look, there are 5,280 feet per mile. If you are traveling 100 miles per hour to avoid stall, that is 528,000 feet per hour. There are 3,600 seconds per hour (60 minutes per hour, times 60 seconds per minute). So, you are traveling at 140 feet per second. So, ignoring angle of attack, of which there isn't any here, if you are 400 feet above the deck, and something goes wrong, which it will, you have less than 3 seconds to keep it in the sky and not in the ground. What about a wind shear? What if kids or whomever run onto the drop zone? What if these big pallets, which we have never dropped before, snag the bomb bay and pull us down? What if the pilot has to sneeze? What if a lot of things.

Everyone was silent for a minute.

More put on his Captain voice, and said, "Yes, what if a lot of things. But, as we say in Montana, what you gotta do, you just gotta do it. So we will, and let those tulips tickle Big Chief's lovely ass."

So we did.

The first run, on May 1, was a piece of cake. No problems from the Germans, no problems with Maps' arithmetic. We flew over (barely over) the marked zone, and saw civilians of all ages crowding the borders, waving, jumping, you could almost hear them shouting and laughing. Our load hit the deck, pieces of pallet flew in all directions, everything bounced, and, as we got out of there, we could see people streaming onto the field. I couldn't tell, really, what they looked like.

We did it so well that the Brass let Big Chief do it again on May 2. Let me tell you about this, because it was the only time I shed tears since I had left home in 1941: As we circled above the drop site before backing off and dropping down for our run in, we could see that the Dutch had taken cutters to a big field of tulips. In good English, and in big, big letters, they had marked out, by cutting off the tops of the tulips, "THANK YOU".

So they let us do it again on May 3, and if this counted as a combat zone mission, it was our 30th, the magic number. We were singing and joking over the intercom as we flew the short distance from base, over the Channel, and thus to northern Holland.

We dropped our load without incidents, veterans in this deal now, and pulled up to head for home.

And then things didn't go so well.

We were just starting to gain a little altitude when there was a loud bang and a flash from the portside wing just behind the number 2 engine. Flames jumped out and spread rapidly, with fuel splashing from torn lines.

I never knew whether there had been some bizarre mechanical dysfunction, or whether some soldier on the ground had fired at us with a Panzerfaust explosive grenade. Most likely the latter, given what proved to be the extent of the damage, and its rapid extension. Within less than Maps' three seconds the entire wing was in flames, and More was shouting to me that he couldn't hold her. Given how close we were to the ground, there was not much we could do. Of course parachutes were out of the question, even if we had had to time to strap them on. More was struggling to keep her nose up and her wings level, but it was a losing proposition. The port wing pulled us over, flames were everywhere, and within seconds, it seemed, we cartwheeled into the ground.

I had braced, but I saw More's head slam forward, and then back. No sound came from him, his head on an un-natural angle on his neck. I heard shouts and screaming from all over the plane, it seemed as if everything inside as well as outside was on fire. My seat was jammed forward against the control panel; I was able, I don't know how, to get out of my belt and kick my way through my side door, tumbling five feet to the ground. There was a snap and a fierce pain in my right leg, and all I could think of was to claw and pull myself as far away from the plane as I could get. Seemingly within seconds, the plane exploded, showering flames, sparks, and debris into the sky.

I must have passed out; my first sensations, however many minutes after that, were agony in my upper right leg and across my shoulders and upper arms, upper chest, and the front of my neck.

The plane was still on fire, with sporadic thumps of small additional explosions and the crackling of machine gun ammunition cooking off.

I passed out again, I don't know for how long. When I came to, the wreck was still afire, but the flames were much lower now, and explosions had ceased. I shouted and shouted for each of my crew mates, but no one responded. And then I went out again, this time for a long time.

The crash must have taken place around noon. When I awoke again, I knew I was alone. I had a raging thirst, a piercing headache, what was undoubtedly a fractured right femur, and severe burns from my upper arms, across my chest, and up into the front of my neck. I had no water, no morphine, no bandages, and no idea what really had happened. My instinct was to crawl as far away from the smoldering wreckage as possible, knowing that the crash would attract searchers, and that they would almost certainly be German soldiers.

When I awoke for the third time, darkness had fallen. I felt my strength, and my will to live, ebbing.

And then I saw flashlights approaching. Like a wounded animal, I pulled and pushed myself, despite the agony in my limbs and chest, further from the plane and towards some low bushes. There was no way that I could fight for my life, but my primitive impulse was to hide and somehow survive.

So they would find me eventually, and, if I was lucky, shoot me.

Four men emerged from the darkness. But they were not German soldiers. They were Dutch Resistance, one of them in his late forties, two in their twenties, and one not yet out of school. They had tracked down the fire, came to see if there were any useful things left, or any still-living Germans they could kill and strip of weapons.

They spoke among themselves in Dutch, but to me in English, and, though they said little, they were extremely kind and gentle as they cared for me. Water, a little food, a rough splint of dubious effectiveness for my right leg. One of them smeared some kind of oily substance over my extensive burns (I think it must have been gun grease). It soothed the burns somewhat, keeping the moving air off them. They had no pain medication to give me.

I remember only snatches of the next three days, as they carried me to the safety of the Allied front lines. I drifted in and out of consciousness, waking to pain and sleeping without dreams, at least not any I remember. I do remember being carried between the four of them in a blanket. I remember being in a wheelbarrow, and somewhere for a short time in a truck. I have no memories of how we crossed the several canals nor of at least one river that I knew lay between our drop site and the Allied lines.

We must have mostly hidden by day, and traveled mostly by night, perhaps sending a scout ahead before moving forward short distances at a time with me. We saw no Germans nor any other person. They knew, as well or better than I, that their lives were forfeit if they were caught with me.

I learned later that on May 5, the day before they delivered me, more dead than alive, to the Yanks, the German Army in the Netherlands had surrendered.

I had assumed that, upon reaching the safety of the Allied Lines, they would remain. But the older one said, "No, we go back to look for our families and our homes, which we have not seen for a long time. And to find any German soldiers left in our land, and kill them."

My war was over. I probably would not have survived my second- and third- degree burns, which were badly infected, were it not for the new sulfa drugs and, later, the miracle of penicillin. I was cared for first at the Battalion Aid Station, for emergency treatment for my dehydration and infection. Then, as soon as possible, I was flown out to the Base Hospital in England, where initial surgery on my fractured femur and associated infection of the bone and hip joint took place, and for repeated skin grafting for my burns. Later, much later, I was flown back to the States, to the Veterans Hospital in Missouri, for more surgeries, rehabilitation, and convalescence. My Mom and Dad, and Betsey, were there to greet me when I arrived. No words of mine can describe that meeting.

I was discharged from the Army in December of 1945. Two weeks later, Betsey and I were married, in Topeka, and our son, Jacob Jr. (universally known as Jake) was born on the Fourth of July, 1947. I hobble around with my cane, but I can still toss the ball back and forth with Jake, and when he is a little bigger we will hit grounders to one another. I am embarrassed, but not ashamed, at my burn scars, but a long- sleeved shirt buttoned right up near my chin keeps most curious glances away.

What I love best of all to do is to go out onto the Prairie, under the starry night sky, and make love to Betsey, in that silent world.

My dreams are troubled, how could they not be? I have two recurrent dreams and one frequently-occurring mental image.

In the first dream, I am standing in the center of a circle, surrounded by my old crew-mates, who stare at me silently. When I approach or address any one of them, he turns his back to me. Then, when I approach or address another, the first one turns around again, and stares at me, silent as before.

In the second dream, I am looking down from the cockpit of the Big Chief. We fly over a blighted landscape of ruins, silent, nothing moving. A Great Sigh emanates from below, and fills my ears, seems to fill the sky.

The vision that I see in my mind's eye is a scene I actually remember from the Veterans Hospital. It is a line of patients, all in wheelchairs, sitting on the sunny veranda of the hospital, all in a straight, silent line, raising their faces to the sun.

FREDDI VERMEER (1954)

My name is Fredrika Brandsma Vermeer, but no one has ever called me anything but 'Freddi.' I will be 50 years old next year, though I feel that I have lived through enough to be 80, and doubt that I will live to reach that age. My father, Karel Brandsma, died during the Hunger Winter a decade ago, of pneumonia and starvation at age 65; my mother, Bertine de Groot, is an embittered and lonely woman of more than 70 years. She still lives, alone with her memories, in the little house near Amersfoort, in the Netherlands, the house in which I was born. I have not seen nor spoken to her in more than four years, and yet my mother took, at a critical point, an action which may have saved the lives of myself and my dear daughter, Christina. During the worst of the Nazi Occupation, after my father died and my mother was starving alone in Amersfoort, she refused to move to our small village, to live with Christina and myself, where we had somewhat more to eat and were able to keep warmer in the terrible times of the *Hongerwinter*. She did this, I believe, because moving might have alerted the German authorities to discover that her own mother, a generation earlier, had been a Jew. That quite likely would have led to my mother, myself, and Christina having been deported to the death camps. An unusual instance of heroism, but, I believe, heroism nevertheless. On such narrow lines were our fates determined during the Occupation.

I married a boy from Amersfoort, Jacob Vermeer, whose family were, like mine, small farmers. Jacob and I were, and always remained, happy with, and devoted to, one another. Like many others of our generation, we wanted a bit more of 'town life', and yet we did not want to lose touch with the land. Jacob's dream was to work on the railroad. All things considered, we moved to the edge of a little village not far from the larger town of Putten, buying a small house with enough land attached to grow vegetables and have a few animals. We worked hard to build a good life for ourselves; we had good neighbors and we were good neighbors. Jacob got a job, starting as a laborer, on the railroad, and worked himself up to a position of Section Head. Our only living child, Christina, was born in 1932, and afterwards we had great difficulty in conceiving another child, which both Jacob and I wanted.

Our lives were quiet, and I suppose you would call them simple, but we were not only content, but happy, with each other and with our lives. We never aspired to wealth, nor really to anything other than what we had. The Great Depression of the 1930's scarcely had any impact upon us.

And then, in 1940, the Germans came, and our lives were turned upside down.

I myself did not quite finish high school, and I have never attempted to put down any sort of record of my life until now. I would ask you to pardon the simplicity of my words and thoughts.

I am moved to do this now, in 1954, from my apartment in Toronto, Canada. Christina has only recently shared with me, for the first time, the account that she wrote back in 1950, just before we left the Netherlands forever and emigrated to Canada. From that account I learned things which I had never known, or had known in a different way.

So it seems to me that I should add my own account to hers, and especially since in this year I have become a grandmother for the first time. Christina and John have a baby girl, sweet Elsa, and I think it is only fitting that Elsa someday have some clear sense of where she comes from, so that she may eventually choose for herself where she is going (Those words are not mine, but rather a version of an old Dutch proverb).

So, back to the invasion of 1940, and the coming of the Germans. This was a complete surprise to us, because of the supposed state of neutrality existing, since before the First Great War, between the Netherlands and Germany. The terror bombing of Rotterdam was a great shock, not only because of the disaster itself, but because it foretold for us what our future would be like. Deliberately choosing to target civilian residential areas, killing hundreds of men, women, and children from the skies, and then following up by parachute and land-based invasion: these were the signals of the brutality that was about to confront us. We were overwhelmed. When the Queen and her family and high advisors fled to Britain by ship, we felt, not without reason, abandoned. Then Belgium was over-run, the British evacuated Dunkirk, and France collapsed, and there seemed to be nothing left of the world as we had known it.

The Germans, who are always so quick and direct and sure of themselves, came into our country and took over, just like that. It seemed like only one day from the next that there was a German officer making the decisions in our village, and reporting to a German officer in Putten, and so on, I suppose, up to Hitler in Berlin. If they asked advice, or even information, from the local or national Dutch officials, many of whom, shamefully, worked on under (and I mean 'under', not 'with') them, I never heard of such. What the Germans were very good at was making noise—clomping boots, banging on doors and tables, shouting orders, ramming engines. And pushing people, pushing people out of the way, pushing people into cars or cells, always pushing. We Dutch are sometimes hard-headed and stubborn when we think we are right, but we are not always pushing. And we do not usually make a lot of noise, except when we are laughing with friends.

But all that was not the most important part. Nor was the fact that our own country was not really our own country anymore, but somebody else's country, even that was not the most important part.

The most important part was the fear. Fear based upon real things—men pulled off the streets or from their homes, never to be seen again. House doors bashed open the middle of the night, fierce dogs barking and snapping and bright flashlights flicking. Husbands and wives dragged off, children left standing in the doorways in their nightshirts. Fear, watching Jews beaten in the streets, forced to scrub the streets on their knees, and then disappearing in their turn, in silence and resignation. Fear that your neighbor was no longer your good neighbor, and would tell tales about you, whether true or not, that might cost you your freedom or your life.

If you have never known such fear, and I pray for you that you never will, you cannot fully understand what it means. It means that you can do nothing, and that 'they' can do anything they wish.

Hate begets hate, and I hated the Germans, because of what they took from Jacob and Christina and myself, and from my mother and father, and from my neighbors and friends, and from all the Dutch people that I did not even know. And, though I am ashamed to say it, I hate them still, though I know it is wrong to do so. And I remain afraid, in ways I never dreamed possible. Now, even safe in Canada, this beautiful and welcoming country, if I hear someone speaking German, I am afraid. And I am ashamed of my fear, and deeply ashamed of my hatred. But what can I do? They took my husband, they took Christina's childhood, they took my father, they took my mother's confidence, they took my friends, they took my country. Just like that. How could I not feel fear? And how could I give up my hate?

With the coming of the Occupation, there was severe privation, of course. Many things were forbidden. Many others were no longer available. We learned to scrimp and save, we learned to stretch things out and put one thing to use as another thing, and we learned to hide and to deceive. The scarcity of shoes, and warm clothing, and tires, and easy travel, we learned to cope with. The increasing scarcity of food, even before the *Hongerwinter* (I still, even now after four years in Canada, find it difficult to call it the Hunger Winter) was harder to bear, but we could cope. But the scarcity of personal freedom, freedom of action and even of thought, was unbearable.

I was a farm girl. Simple, but I knew how to make things work, one way or another. I knew that things did not always turn out the way one wanted them to. I knew how to keep trying until they did. I knew that good things came from the earth and the sun, and that you should give good things back. I knew that Jacob felt the same way, and that this was our strength together.

And then, suddenly, it was not enough, and the world was a truly evil and dangerous place, and so I was afraid. And Jacob, though he would never say so, or give in to it, was afraid as well.

Of all my fears, two were the greatest. One was that Jacob would be taken from me. Many, many Dutch wives and parents had this fear come to pass. Because it often happened suddenly and without warning, and away from your presence, and then forever, it was difficult not to feel this fear at every moment, constantly. What could I say each morning at the doorstep when I handed Jacob his lunch sack? Come back to me this evening? Don't let them take you today? See you for dinner?

Of course there was good reason, I knew, for this fear. From early on, Jacob worked in the Resistance. I do not know, to this day, what that actually meant, what he actually did (beyond meeting secretly with others, men and women as well), or even clearly when he did it. Despite my fear, I was glad, and I was proud of him.

And then, of course, that debt to fear had to be paid, and was. When the Railway strike began, he was implicated, and had to flee 'for his life' in the night. After he was gone, I never knew, and still do not know, the rest. Not a word, not a sign, not a message, not a notification. Not during the last months of the Resistance and the War, not during the *Hongerwinter*, not during Liberation, not when leaving the Netherlands, not now in Canada. I am never to know which of my nightmares became the reality.

My second great fear was that something dreadful would befall Christina. The Germans, to give the devils their due, were not often abusive to Dutch women, and Christina was still, physically, a child right through until Liberation and beyond, but of course a mother still worries. There were still so many ways, by accident or by innocence, that she could have fallen into danger. She could have said or done the 'wrong' thing. She could have stepped into the street in front of a German car with the usual heavy-footed driver. She could, as Christina would, have defended the wrong friend, Jew or otherwise. When I learned, years after the Occupation, that she had carried and posted Resistance flyers when she was 'Going to the Farms', my heart stopped beating for a moment.

Most likely, of course, she and I could have been swept up if Jacob were exposed and arrested.

After Jacob disappeared, I thought things were going to end for Christina and myself. When no word or rumor followed, at first I did not think we could carry on. And then, after a while, when we were not arrested, I began to see that as long as we were allowed to live, that Jacob might be still free. Had he been taken, they probably would have come for us. So, for a time, I was reassured because there was no word, reassured that he was out there and alive, somewhere. And then I realized that there might have been no word if Jacob were dead.

We all knew, from early on, what the jails were like, what the detention camps were like, what the sealed trains were about, what the extermination camps were for. There were no secrets here.

It is a strange thing about fear such as we experienced during the Occupation: when the cause of the fear is over, even long over, the fear really never disappears. It can come back to strike you with the lightning flash of memory. It can come at any time, at any moment. It can come from anywhere, even from something that one would think was completely innocent, such as the song of a particular bird.

I should say something about the Hunger itself. Something besides how difficult it was. I think that the Hunger had two faces. One was up very close, staring into your eyes. You wanted food, how you wanted it, and you wanted it now, and again, every instant. It hurt, not like a knife which is there and then gone, but like a badly broken bone, which hurts and hurts and hurts. This was always there, through all the months of the *Hongerwinter*.

The other face of the Hunger was the dead face. You were so tired. Not tired like after a hard climb up a hill. Just tired, weary, not wanting to take another step, say another word, think another thought. Tired in a way that rest could not relieve. At times you just wanted the Hunger to end, even if that meant that then everything would end.

The two faces of Hunger were not opposites. They were both always there, together. They filled your attention, and demanded your concession. The only respite was finding food. Or death.

It was my pregnancy that helped me resist. Jacob and I had so wanted another child, a brother or sister for Christina. I was glad that Jacob knew of my pregnancy before he left us; I knew that this would give him strength in whatever trials he faced. And it gave me strength to keep myself going, to find food, to send my Christina to The Farms, despite the risks.

When my time came, it was so easy, despite any weakness of mine. It was another way to defeat the two Hungers, and to defy the power of the Germans over us.

The baby was small but well-formed and initially vigorous. I was surprised to find that my milk was plentiful, despite my starved body. For about 4 days he fed hungrily.

And then, he just faded away. Faded away. He never even had time to know his name, which would of course have been Jacob. Perhaps, sometimes I think, he and Jacob are somewhere together.

Three things saved me then, in that terrible time after my little one died. The first was Christina, and I will tell you more about her later. The second was Jacob, though he was not there. And the third was my neighbor, Elsa (whose name my granddaughter now bears).

Elsa, my neighbor I mean, had carried through a difficult pregnancy, and delivered her baby boy just a week or so before I went into labor. Her husband, a friend and co-worker of my Jacob's on the railroad, had been too slow to dive when the strike started. He was taken by the Nazis, and beaten to death in a cell in Putten. They would not give her the body, but word leaked back to Elsa from the Resistance.

Without her husband, getting food was even harder for Elsa, and she was profoundly starved. Nevertheless, her child was born and seemed healthy. But Elsa's milk was thin and meager, and it was clear that the child, like many others, had little chance of survival.

So, still having my milk, but no child of mine to feed, I did what any good Dutch neighbor would do: I went over to Elsa's house three or four times a day, and suckled the boy. And that was his survival. And that was my survival as well, both the happiest and saddest thing I ever did.

Christina and I leaned on each other. I know now that the year of the Hongerwinter damaged us both, in ways some of which we knew, and some of which chase behind us to this day though we don't understand them fully. As close as we were (and are), there was, as there is in all persons who are starving (for food or whatever else): a certain distance, an empty space filled only by the Self, who cares only for getting what it needs and does not have, more and more and more of it.

I had lived a very normal and simple life before the Occupation, and so had that as a base of strength to measure against the privations and even the fear. But, as you learned from what Christina said in her story from 1950, she had no such base of strength. Everything began, for her, when the Germans came. Where the Occupation was a storm that overturned the life I had known, for Christina the Occupation WAS her life, up to the time of Liberation.

I am so proud of Christina's courage. She was, truthfully, Jacob's daughter, and I think he knew that. It wasn't just in her 'Going to the Farms'. It was in her never giving in, never, never. When we did not have nearly enough, she would say, "Mamma, we will get more tomorrow."

After the Allies saved us from starvation, and drove the Germans away, it was Christina who pulled me out of darkness. Together we rebuilt our lives. I watched her become a young woman. She and I were truly friends.

It is due to Christina that we came here to Canada. Way back in 1946, less than a year after Liberation, we received a letter from Jacob's elder brother, who had emigrated to a far-off place called Toronto during the 1930's. Now, married and with children of his own, he was seeking to know whether we had survived and, if so, how we were faring.

I was at a low point at that time, and probably would not even have opened the letter. But Christina did, and replied, and so a correspondence developed between her and them. When the Canadian Vermeers proposed, in 1948, that we join them in the New World, I would never have had the energy or curiosity to go.

But Christina saw it, as she saw most things, as a life-changing opportunity. So, in 1950, Christina and I bid our old lives good-bye, boarded a ship, and crossed the ocean. Christina had just graduated from High School.

And how right she was, at least for her. Christina has bloomed here, in all the ways a mother could have wished. And now she has her John, and we all have our Elsa.

As for me, well, the change has been good for me as well, but there are wounds that cannot be mended. I suppose I am a woman elderly beyond my years, stockings a little baggy, sometimes even muttering to herself in the street.

There is one more story I must tell you.

One day in July, back there in 1945, when we were all recovering, trying to live again, only several months after the Germans left, I heard, or perhaps felt, a strange procession moving slowly down the village street. There came a procession of perhaps forty men: ragged and thin beyond comprehension. They walked in silence. Most ragged of all was their footwear, tattered soles and pieces of uppers, held together by rags and twine. They looked as if they formed a pilgrim group of survivors fleeing the plague or some catastrophe of centuries ago. One man had only one shoe; his other foot was bound in rags. As they came through the village, he stopped, removed his shoe, and switched shoe and rags each to the opposite foot; then he shuffled on.

Who were these silent men? Perhaps they were the few survivors of the slave labor deportees taken by the Germans from Putten. Perhaps not.

I rushed into the house and called Christina to help me. We carried out all the water we could find, and all the food that we had, and distributed these to the gaunt and silent men. They nodded their thanks of acceptance, and then moved on their way.

It was at that moment, once and forever, that I knew I would never see my Jacob again.

CHRISTINA VERMEER-EVANS
(1954)

When I read and re-read my mother's account, I am most struck by two things. First, her undying love for my father and for me, something I suppose a child takes for granted until proven otherwise, which is, sadly, all too often the case. And second, the depth of the torment, fear, and, yes, hatred that the Occupation experience left, and still leaves, within her.

I have waited several months before putting down my own reactions to her thoughts, wanting to place them in comparison with my own feelings. Of course, in the four years we have been in Canada, my life has taken a trajectory that I can only label as 'blessed'. To come from the shattered Netherlands of 1945, through the sparse and difficult time of our personal and national recovery; to find myself at the age of 18 in a new and magical world in Canada, where people were not only safe, but happy; to grow into the Christina that I wanted to be, rather than the Christina that I had had to be. And then, to find and marry John and, merely months ago, to be blessed with my own daughter, Elsa: my Fourth Life has been, to say the least, worth waiting and struggling for.

My mother's comments about fear and hate gave me much to think about. My conclusion is that there are some wounds which never heal. But what becomes of those who bear them?

So I asked myself, as honestly as I could, do I still fear the Germans, and do I hate them? The answer to the first question is a clear No. I did fear them, terribly, as a child. But I am no longer a child, and they have no longer any power over me, or over my dreams. I have beaten them.

My dreams are of flying across the polders on my bicycle. 'Going to the Farms'. Not of barking dogs nor weeping or disappearing people. At least, not very often.

Do I hate them? This is more difficult, because I did hate who and what they were, and what they did to me and mine. And if I myself can change as I have, can they change as well, and is there room for redemption, and for forgiveness, in this world? But what evil they brought into my world still exists, and will continue to exist, in many places, and I now have Elsa to think about. When she reads these words, many years from now, she will have to answer these questions for herself. For me, it is still too close to the bone, and I have no answer, for myself or others.

When the War and the Occupation ended, my mother and I rebuilt our lives, keeping the memories of the missing pieces alive, but trying to look always forward. We had a small pension from my father's work, the social support programs from the Dutch government were adequate, my mother found work as a shop assistant, and I found ways for short-term work after school and on school vacations. We had our snug little house, and slightly more than the 'bare necessities.' We were not alone; there were many, many women-only households in the Netherlands in the first years after the

War. I enjoyed school and friends, but like some of the children I knew, especially those who had lost a parent, or grandparents, I was somewhat reserved, and kept many of my thoughts to myself. As time moved on, our little village settled back into a quiet life; we did not experience the short period of sometimes-violent retribution and reprisals against those who had collaborated with the Nazi's, though there were some in the village who we felt were forever no longer really among us. Though their lives must have become terrible indeed, most of them stayed where they had always been. Where else could they go?

For all of us, including my mother and myself, what was lost was lost, and never to be forgotten, but life moved on. For me, as I moved through my teens, there was sometimes a strange space, neither past nor present, but not yet future. That all changed for me when we came to Canada, not as if one door had been closed, but as if one had opened.

Strangely enough, we never really re-established a close connection with my grandmother, despite the fact that we both believed she may well have saved our lives. But Grandmother sunk further and further into isolation: angry, bitter, and depressed. She seldom left her house, and would not come to visit us, let alone to live with us. I think that, just as there are some wounds which do not heal, there are some that fester, boring deep into the mind and soul.

When, only a year after the end of the War, I began a correspondence with my uncle and aunt and cousins in Canada, I had no thought that it would change my life. At first, I think, that the arrival of the initial letter from my father's brother was for me a link to his memory. But their kindness knew no bounds, even to their sending packages of useful gifts to us, the only 'presents' I could recall since I was eight years old, apart from those I had received from my parents.

And when my aunt, whom I had never met, and whose own parents had died in the Netherlands during the Occupation, gently raised the idea of my mother and I coming to live in Canada, there was no way my mind could conceive of what that reality might entail.

My mother did not want to go. She had the anchors of her past life, before the Germans came. For her there was a 'before' and an 'after', and she was afraid to give up the 'before'. For me, there was only an 'after', and to let that go was to risk losing all.

But, in the end, it was my mother who was the one who saw the Opportunity, the chance for her daughter if not for herself. She says it was me who saw the Opportunity, but I know it was really her, though she denies it.

And so, though it took almost three years to decide and then to complete arrangements, in 1950 we boarded ship and passed to a new life.

Before we left the Netherlands, there was one thing that I felt I must do. Almost 18, I took my adult-sized bicycle, carrying a basket full of small gifts, and 'Went to the Farms' once again. I tried to find each farm family that, seemingly so long ago, had offered me shelter or food, and also each farm from which I had stolen. There were many who, or whose locations, I could not remember. There were some who did not remember me. There were undoubtedly some who were the 'wrong' ones. I was 'At the Farms' for 5 days, and given shelter and food once again, as I had been years before. No one turned me away. When I thanked them, most thanked me for remembering them.

Our Dutch-Canadian relatives in Toronto welcomed us, helped us (including financially) to settle, and to adjust to a strange and different culture, far different than anything either of us had known.

Mother and I lived together in a small apartment, and she found work as the secretary for a small import-export company owned by a Dutch couple who had come to Canada in 1938; they were Jews from Amsterdam who had seen what was coming; none of the relatives they had left behind had survived the camps.

My mother's English was adequate, but not so good as mine, and because of that and other reasons, she had difficulty moving outside the local Dutch community. For her, life in Canada was a Fourth Life: Life in the Netherlands before the Occupation, Life during the Occupation, Life in the Netherlands after the War, and now life in a far-away land, from which she looked mostly to the past. It was, in a way, easier for her to move further into isolation, and I am not sure I was of as much help to her as she had been to me during my Lives. I regret that, and what can only be described as a kind of selfishness as I explored my new, magical, almost fairy-tale existence.

Though my English, like most Dutch people, was excellent (despite the 5 years when it was forbidden to be spoken in school during the Occupation), I decided it was wiser to not try and go on to University for a few years, and rather to seek work that would acculturate me faster, make me "more Canadian". I told myself that this was the time for me to once again 'Go to the Farms', in a manner of speaking, and that what I had done once, I could do again.

Our apartment was near the University and the Medical School, and I was fortunate enough, after about 6 months, to secure a job in the University Library System. Nothing could have been better in all respects: it helped my language and my identity, and it put me in daily contact with young people. It was a minor job, mostly filing and categorizing and shelving books and journals; I worked hard and the work never seemed boring. Each day I felt more Canadian and less Dutch, and at times I felt a bit guilty about that, especially as time went on and there was less and less to talk about with my mother.

I began to make friends, and even to take whatever advantages I could of the cosmopolitan environment of Toronto.

One morning, in early 1952, I was in the Medical Library, at the front desk, preparing books and journals for shelving, when a youngish physician came up to the desk with a routine question. He must have noticed my accent, because he asked me where I was from. "From the Netherlands, where the Dutch are," I replied.

"That's interesting, my father was a medical officer with the First Canadian Army at the battle for the Scheldt, and he always speaks of how warm and welcoming the Dutch were to us", Dr. John Evans said.

I directed him to the location of the medical journal he was seeking.

The next day, the same young doctor, but in a freshly-pressed white coat, came back to the reference desk again, this time with a less obvious question. And the next day he was back again, though he must have had to inquire, or search, for which library I was working at that day.

And in quite rapid but due course, we went out for coffee, then for dinner, then to the movies, and so forth and so on and so very well. We were married in early 1953, and our daughter, Elsa Vermeer-Evans, was born in this year of 1954.

Such a long way it has been from the terror bombing of Rotterdam!

PART TWO:
THIS WITHERED LAND

MATTHEW RILEY (1960)

My name is Matthew Riley, though I know not how I came by either part of it; probably by the village priest who found me, newly born, at the church font. I was a lone and misbegotten Irish boy, all, all alone in County Cork, put on this earth in 1869, less than 20 years after the Great Potato Famine, when the Bloody English starved a million of us to death, to take our land, and to drive other millions from the Auld Sod and scatter us to the winds.

During the first ten years of what might be called my childhood, in the Foundling Home and later the Orphanage, life for all of us was hard. Some became hard and faithless with it, but some, including me, by God's Grace, looked to find a better life, and a better world.

At about age 10 (for the day and month of my birth remain unknown to me) I was taken from the Orphanage by a childless farmer and his wife, and set to work on the saltwater farm. I was worked hard, and beaten harder, but at least I had a straw pallet of my own, and, for the first time, enough to eat.

The farmer's wife taught me to read. Some winters, when the fields were fallow, I attended a bit of school.

And then, at age 15, I saw my Opportunity, and, as I have always done, took it.

I ran, by night and by day, with but one thought in my head: America.

And now, aged 91, I am dying. I have lived a full life and, I hope, a good one, and I am looking forward to seeing Edna, my wife and love of my life, who crossed over only three years ago.

From such a hard start as I have had, life has been good to me, and I put this down to three things: the least is my own talents, such as they have been. The second is God's Grace, which has never failed me. And the third is the United States of America, which has gifted this poor boy with Freedom.

Now, dying in 1960, I shall die in the very same year that an American-Irish Catholic lad will, I trust, be elected President of these United States. I would like to live long enough to cast my precious vote for him, but I doubt that I will be able to.

Imagine! Imagine what the story of my life tells, and may you see in it the possibilities for your own.

I have paid America back for the Freedom and bounty she has bestowed on me. I gave my younger son, Ernie, to the U.S Marine Corps, to be shot to death by the Japs at age 19, on some island whose name hardly anyone knows. And my older son, Jacob, I gave to the Army Air Corps, to come home from Europe no longer a smiling boy, but rather a worn, crippled, and inward-looking man. But, at least, he has come home to us.

So let me tell you how I came to this Blessed Land.

Quite simply: by grit and by guile.

I ran, as I said. Across the fields, where I shivered, and through the Cities, where I begged and stole.

I made my way to Southampton, in that bleak and cursed England, and haunted the docks where the great Ocean Liners waited. I had a chance to do a favor, to save a poor family of, believe it or not, Romanian Jews, from robbery. The husband and wife, and their infant daughter, were almost, but not quite, as poor as I was, and had spent most of what they had on passage to New York. Their initial goal had been for South Africa, but they hadn't enough for that, just enough for America. In gratitude, they passed me off as their own child (the father, Solomon, had hair as red as mine) and there I was, in steerage aboard the coal-burning SS Saint Paul, bound from Southampton to New York.

Getting through the Immigration at New York was more difficult, even worse than the long voyage, but let me just say that stealth, cunning, and a bit of the Irish blarney, found me on the better side of the barrier, winking back at Officer O'Brien. I bid God Speed to Solomon and Anna, whom I never saw again, but whom I have thanked every morning and evening of my life since, and turned my face to the West.

I worked my way, doing a bit of this and of that. But, though I slept where I could lay down, and ate when I could, I never stole again. Never.

It was in the wild farmlands of New Jersey or Pennsylvania, somewhere in there, that it came to me. All of 16, I was in a sort of a bar, having a beer with a fellow for whom I had spent a week working with him on his land. As folks will do in that sort of situation, he turned to a fellow farmer. "You see this lad, here, Jack? He has some Gift that makes him able to do, or fix, or build, anything at all. Give him two pieces of any kind and shape, and he will make something of it that works, and probably moves. It's a Gift he has, that and able to talk the birds out of the trees. And, well, of course, like you and me, he's Irish."

Well, if I say so myself, it was mostly true. I always have had that Gift. Perhaps it comes from having had to always make something out of nothing, whether in the Foundling Home, the Orphanage, the Farm, or on my Journey. It didn't always work, but mostly it did.

And that gave me the Idea. I begged a broken old wood cart from my employer, banged it together with some wood slats into a hand truck, and using some spare black paint, lettered on the one side "Mick the Fix-It-Man", and on the other, "If It Don't Work, I Pay You."

Picking up old discarded tools and such as I went, I kept my face turned to the West, and so I made my way along, fixing things that people broke.

Broken tools and instruments? No problem, I could always find a local smith to allow me to stand at his forge, and pay him back with an hour's work at whatever. A bashed and dented hat? Easy, as long as it was near my own size, and the owner had a teakettle to make steam. And so on and so forth. I had to pay more than a few times, but I earned my wage, and often my keep, more than I needed to survive.

So I made my way, free as the breeze: New Jersey, Pennsylvania, Ohio, Illinois, Missouri, and to Kansas. It was scarcely more than 20 years since the Great War for Freedom ended, and thousands were on the roads, some poor, a few rich, all looking for their future, whether they came from next door or from across the ocean. I had my troubles, which were few, and my Freedom, which was all I needed.

I was about 18, lean and strong, when I reached Topeka, Kansas. And there I met my Edna. She was working as a maid to a Lady. She always claimed to be one-quarter Cherokee Indian, but I think at least some of that was Negro, which made her to me all the more beautiful, and all the more American. And I met her, Truth is, in Church.

Let me explain. I had learned, as I traveled, that a good place to find people who had things to fix was outside of Churches. Families were gathered there, Sunday was a day to stop and talk, and my sign (by now I had a small covered wagon and a mule), still drew attention. So I would set up outside the church and then, of course go inside (I blush to say that, though I am a Catholic to this day, I did not draw distinction as to which establishment was handy).

So, in the year 1887, I had met my Edna, an orphan like myself, and we knew we would never leave each other. I sold my wagon and mule and tools, and went to work in the Topeka stockyards, where the cattle were driven in before being transported on the railroads. It occurred to me that their journeys East were quite a bit faster than mine West had been.

It was hard and dirty work, but I was young and knew how to do that. I made no trouble, fought only when I had to, used my brain when it was required, and by 1889 I was made a sort of foreman.

Edna and I could walk out together, and her Lady took a liking to us both, so that of an evening, when work was done, I could come and sit with Edna in the kitchen.

It was Edna who first had the idea, who first learned that on April 22, 1889, the United States Government was going to give away land, free to who came first (except for the Indians, whom they had driven from the land, in the area called Oklahoma Territory, or

"Indian Territory"). They had stolen the land, and now they were going to give it to whoever wanted to live on and work it.

It was called 'The Great Land Rush', and people were to stand at a line and then at noon on the day, rush to claim a section, anywhere they wanted.

Edna said that, since she was part Cherokee, she deserved a little special treatment, and so we, along with many others who came to be called "Sooners", gave ourselves a bit of an edge. I went out a night or two before the Great Day, and hid myself along a nice creek of running water on the prairie (that Edna and I had scouted out some weeks before). Edna waited in the proper place, with the borrowed horses, and, when the bugle blew, rode Hell for Leather directly out to me, and that was that. Two cast-offs, without many pennies between us—Land Owners. In America!

It could be harsh, but it was Heaven to us, on the Prairie. Our first house was one bare room of sod ('peat' they would have called it in the Old Country). Winters we froze and Summers we broiled. Rain, snow, wind, drought, locusts. It would have broken either one of us but for the love of the other. And the beauty of the Prairie, when it wasn't trying to kill you. I can say that our fifteen years or more on the Prairie was the happiest time of our lives.

The farm (one could scarcely call it a ranch) was hardscrabble. The creek, often mostly dry by mid-summer, and frozen solid by late November, had, I always said, a funny odor to it, oily-like.

And that, with the luck I've always had, was it. Turned out we were indeed sitting on a puddle, a very large puddle, of oil. Some fellers about broke down our door arguing about who could give us the most for our land and oil rights, and, in 1915, with more money than we had ever thought existed, we moved back to Topeka.

Well, we bought the big house, too big for us since we had not had children on the Prairie, though we tried. I had the money, and once again saw Opportunity and took it. Automobiles were the coming thing, so I bought the first Ford Agency in town: sales, parts, repairs. And then added automotive farm equipment to it. And within a few years, mechanical things were taking to the skies. Topeka got in early as the aircraft manufacturing center of the country, believe it or not ("The Airline Capitol of the World" it staged itself in those years), and I got into the airplane supply and parts business early myself. My 'Gift' was as useful as ever; I kept my hand in and even patented one or two little improvements myself.

And, to top it all off, along came my sons, Jacob in 1921, and Ernie 1924. They were good boys and there was always laughter in the big house. I shall say no more about them, for even now the loss of them both, of Ernie entirely, and of Jacob in what he was, is too painful. Perhaps, I sometimes think, one has to Pay the Piper, and I have had to pay for all the fortune that has smiled on me, and on Edna.

When my Edna passed away, without pain or wasting, these three years ago, at age 85, it was a great sadness, but I was not desolated. For I knew that she would not have long to wait for me, and I am confident that we shall be together again, very, very soon now.

And there is one more great boon that has been granted me. For thirteen years now, in the afternoon and twilight of my life, I have had my Grandson, Jake, the one who refuses to be called Jacob Jr, the one of all of them who comes closest to truly having the 'Gift'. And Jake has me, the one he insists on calling 'The Old Man', which I am, and which name pleases me greatly, though it irritates Jake's father, my son Jacob.

It is said that key parts of inheritance sometimes skip a generation, and I believe that is so with me and Jake. He has my (formerly) red hair, and my way of putting people at ease. He has my way of loving all the good things on this Earth without prattling on about it. He has, almost but not completely, the 'Gift', though perhaps he will grow into it. He is my Twin, though a few years younger. He was born on the Fourth of July, and since, because no one knows when it was, I can choose my own day and month of birth, we have the same Yankee Doodle Birthday.

It is getting late, and dark, and my eyes are tired, but there is one more thing I must tell you before I go. I was just about ready to.........

JAKE RILEY (NOVEMBER, 1982)

I was indeed born on the Fourth of July, in 1947, and whether or not I am a 'Real Live Nephew of My Uncle Sam', I am the Grandson of 'The Old Man', my Grandpa, Matthew Riley, whom I loved above all things on this Earth, and whom I try my damnedest to live up to and emulate in all ways, be they good or bad or in-between.

Not that I didn't have real parents, or grow up in their love and caring; I was lucky or blessed in that way as well. My Mom, Betsey Riley, seemed to me, growing up in the Fifties, sort of like Doris Day—always up, always there, and always on my side. My Dad was another story: harder to be easier with, sort of in a shell, not much smiling going on, but solid as a rock when you needed him. By school-age, I figured out that it was the War that had done it, that and his bad leg and burn scars. He and I both loved baseball, and I loved him hitting fly balls and hot grounders to me, as soon as I got old enough to throw accurately enough back to him without him having to chase them very far.

Among the red-headed Rileys (me, The Old Man, and my Dad), my hair was the reddest, and only I had the freckles, and I had the temperament to go with them. I was pretty determined, some even called me pig-headed. As soon as I was old enough to know the difference, I announced in no uncertain terms that I was NEVER to be called 'Jacob Junior' or 'Little Jacob', or Jacob anything, but that I would only answer to 'Jake.' And so I have, even changed my name legally, so it could go as 'Jake NMI Riley' on my dog tags in the Service ('NMI' is the Army's way of spelling 'No Middle Initial').

My Dad never wanted to talk about the War, but I loved to listen to The Old Man's Tales, about surviving as an orphan in Ireland, coming to America and working his way West on his own, about his and my Gramma Edna's life on the Lone Prairie, about Indians (Gramma always said she was one-quarter Cherokee, and I believe to this day she was) and wild characters and wilder horses, and big storms and dry summers and the disappearance of the free Red Men. Gramma could make an unending supply of lemonade and chocolate chip cookies, which she told me were staples for life on the Lone Prairie.

So I grew up with as much or more of the typical American boy's fixation on adventure, looking over the next hill, and finding what you could do with what you had, no matter what anyone else tried to tell you. Served me well, I guess. Or vice versa; maybe I served those things well.

I did ok in school, but spent a lot of time looking out the window.

Until he died when I was thirteen, The Old Man took me fishing and bird hunting out on the Prairie as soon as I was old enough, which was about eight years old. But what I was really addicted to was anything that had wheels and went fast, and faster was better, and fastest was best.

By the time I was in High School, my other interests were focused on baseball and girls, not necessarily in that order, and, of course, the wheels-and-fast thing helped with the girls thing. Our yard around the big house in Topeka was littered with old cars and parts thereof and motorcycles (ditto).

I survived High School without too many scars, and entered, without real conviction, the University of Kansas at Lawrence, where I kept up my pursuit of wheels and girls, and played Third Base on the Freshman Team. I left K.U. after two years, my departure regretted by none save perhaps the Baseball Coach, who was losing a good third-baseman.

It was Spring of 1968 when I left K.U., and both U.S military involvement and popular opposition to the Vietnam War were increasing to new highs. I wasn't sure whether I was pro or con. But it was pretty clear that my draft number was going to be called sooner rather than later, and so I needed to figure out what I was going to do.

My Mom and especially my Dad were very opposed to the War. I had no great interested in being drafted and being sent to Vietnam, probably as combat infantry. So when I found out that, if I enlisted for a four-year hitch in the Army, I would have some choice as to what I might be doing, I went ahead and did just that: enlisted for a four-year hitch and was able to get training and assignment to a Motor Transport Division as a truck driver. As it turned out, I did my time in Nam anyway, actually two one-year tours, separated by a year Stateside, but saw no direct combat, though the results, and sometimes the sights and sounds, of that were around me all the time.

Actually, I was bored to tears, even during my time overseas, because, despite what the Recruiters told me, I did not often get to "fix 'em as well as drive 'em" and because the driving part for the four years was mostly in endless convoys or back and forth trawling around Army bases. But Truth is, I learned a lot about mechanical things, and about myself, in that time.

When I got out in 1971, I had made sergeant, was 24 years old, and considered myself a very competent driver of anything with wheels, and a damn good auto-mechanic.

I went back home to Topeka, found that all the friends I had had were now somewhere else, and that I had absolutely no idea of what I wanted to do with myself. Dad had taken over the business when The Old Man died in 1960, and he had kept it very successful, which was good for him in many ways. He and I picked up our old ground-ball-hitting style relationship, which had disappeared in my teen-age days. Dad wanted me to come in the business with him, learn it from the ground up, and eventually, though unspoken, take it over. A settled life in Topeka, Kansas, as a local businessman, was about as attractive to me as going back to Vietnam, but I had no other remote idea of what I wanted to do, and did not want to disappoint Mom and Dad, so I agreed, as long as I could focus on the Service and Repairs part, rather than on sales or management.

So there was this kind of unspoken tension, struggle really, between me and Dad, and, actually between me and myself. It eased a bit when I persuaded him to bring in a line of motorcycles for sales and service that I would manage, but I began to see that the life laid out for me was never going to work. Here I was, still living at home in the big house at twenty-seven or so, though I had plenty of social life, and plenty of time for long cycle rides to Nowhere.

It was 1974, and life was passing me by. Or, rather, I was passing myself by. I went to work on my oldest and biggest bike, got it into super shape, and told my Folks I was taking off to, as The Old Man used to say, "See the elephant." Mom got teary but didn't say much. To my great surprise, Dad put his arms around me and told me that he never regretted for an instant his decision to fly airplanes, but was only sorry at the way the breaks had turned out in the end.

So I headed off, with the vague destination of 'Alaska and Wherever Else' in my mind. For the next 4 years, in Alaska, Montana, Wyoming, and California, I was never bored or lonesome. There were plenty of girls in Wherever Else, and Wherever Else I landed there was always work to be found for someone with my vehicle repair and maintenance skills and experience. I wasn't wild or trouble-minded, I was a good and solid worker. If I say so myself, I had an easy way with people that both they and I seemed to like. I just always needed, after a time, to be looking over and past the next hill.

But when the 'next hill' turned out to be my early thirties, I realized I needed a plan, firm plan, for my future. So, after my own fashion, and with a large dose of self-gratification, I designed one.

Here was The Plan, designed to do what I could with what I had, and at the same time retain something of the style of The Old Man: I would use my modest savings to finance air travel (one way) from Kansas City to London. There, I would find the way to get the proper documents I would need to do short- and especially long-haul trucking around the United Kingdom, and then, around Europe. The Plan would take me around the world, but I did not want to do it via well-plowed ground, I wanted to see the edges and by-ways, and take my time. So, I would make my way across the Mediterranean Sea, to Egypt or somesuch, and work long-haul trucking to take me, by stages, down to East Africa, probably Mombasa in Kenya. From Mombasa, or wherever, I would take ship, maybe working my passage, maybe not, to somewhere around India, and get back into trucking work, making my way across Asia and, according to no fixed time schedule, finishing up in Japan. From there I would fly back to the States, and then see what happened next.

Some Plan, eh! But it actually worked, at least the first part. When I got to London, I was able to get the appropriate documents on the basis of my extensive experience, a short course certification, and passing an easy (for me) written and (Left-hand as well as Right-hand drive) road test.

For the next four years or so (My life seemed to come in four-year bits. Maybe it was the Army.), I worked around the United Kingdom and Western Europe, mostly legally, and found my way around the motor transport fraternity. I did a little bit of shadow work in and out of Eastern Europe, and several ferry hauls with who-knows-what between Morocco and France. Then, just like The Old Man said it always did, Opportunity appeared, and an Irish friend in a London pub told me that an organization called Canada Child Survival was looking for experienced long-haul drivers to support their relief work in Ethiopia. Wow—that was almost to Mombasa, give or take a thousand miles! So I contacted their London office, displayed my bona fides in a few short interviews, and had my record and experience checked.

And so here I am, dictating this to myself, on November 25, 1982, on Ethiopian Airlines, with a one-way paid ticket to Addis Ababa.

ELSA VERMEER-EVANS
(NOVEMBER, 1982)

When I was growing up, I never thought of myself as anything but an All-Canadian Girl:

"Oh, Canada" ('My Home and Native Land...'), and, later, Anne Murray's "Snowbird", and, still later, Gordon Lightfoot's "In the Early Mornin' Rain.. And of course, Gordie Howe, 'Mr. Hockey', even if he played for the Detroit Red Wings. And when the Major League Toronto Blue Jays came along, just 5 years or so ago, I was over the moon, even if I was 23 years old. I love baseball, always have, always will.

I learned hardly a word of Dutch, and of course the closest thing I have to a Canadian accent is the Ontario "Eh!" This compromised my relationship with my Grandmother, Freddi, whose English seemed to get less each year, and who, frankly, I hardly know in any intimate way. My Mom, Christina, kept her Dutch accent, which just made her, I think, seem more beautiful and poised, but the language in the Evans household was strictly English.

My icon was my Dad, John Evans. Raised in a classical Anglo-Canadian family that had been in Canada for a hundred years, prospering greatly with the development of the Canadian Railways and the news media, John had the Silver Spoon, but never let it spoil him. He followed his father into medicine, as I followed him in turn. From the time I was a nipper, I trailed around after him, and in some ways, "learned medicine (or at least what it was about) at the stirrup", as the old saying went. My father, a "Prince among men, but with the common touch", encouraged me in every way, and it was clear to me before I started school that I would become, like him, a physician.

When my father died suddenly, in 1968, of a cerebral hemorrhage, my mother and I were devastated. I was fourteen years old. My mother had never immersed me in the history of her own childhood in the Netherlands during and after the Second World War, and, for reasons that I myself do not understand, I never pressed her for the details, though I had some sense of the generalities, which were awful enough.

But somehow, the fact that my father's and her husband's death had taken place at roughly the same stage of early adolescence as her own (Christina's) loss of her own father during the Hunger Winter in the Netherlands, brought us, mother and daughter, closer together than ever before. For me, for the first time, this increased closeness and mutual loss created a strong desire to learn about my mother's adolescence and the associated family history in the Netherlands.

On my mother's part, it is my belief that the primary reason she had not steeped me earlier in the details of the Occupation and the Hunger Winter was her conviction that the story was so horrific that it would damage me in some way. To this day, even though that now, as a Pediatrician, I am supposedly somewhat knowledgeable concerning child psychiatry and child development, I am not at all sure whether she was correct or not.

And so, in 1968, through long and painful discussions, I learned the detailed family history, and was able to read Christina's journal and take in her point of view. We were both mindful of the fact that I was now just a few years older than my mother was when she was 'Going to the Farms'.

That is why I am writing this down now, after long reflection, at age twenty-eight. If I ever get around to it, and have a child or children of my own, I will want them to know where they come from, and how they got to wherever it is that they are.

In addition to bringing us even closer together following my father's death, the story of my Dutch family provoked in me, not only new images of myself, but wider thinking about what the world was. How could such things as the Hunger Winter have happened? What were we, as humans, who could both carry out, and endure, such things? What were our abilities, and responsibilities, to avoid recurrence, or, actually continuation?—for I now saw the world I lived in in a harsher and more realistic light.

All this, I hope, made greater sense of my desire to become a physician; but were there not also larger and even more effective ways to reduce suffering than 'simply' the physical treatment of one's patients' physical symptoms?

Part of this, I realize now, was adolescent idealism, part the journey of self-discovery. But, I think, part was also a sort of 'survivor's guilt.'

And so, my life journey into adulthood began to take shape as a mingled inheritance from both my father AND my mother. What more could one ask for?

I sailed through my undergraduate years at the University of Toronto, and then on through medical school. I was drawn to

Pediatrics, and especially to those children from broken homes and broken lives.

Two patients seen early in my career have stayed with me as lodestones.

The first was the very first patient I saw on my first day as a Third Year medical student on the Pediatric Ward. The Resident said, "Come on, I want you to see this."

The two-year old boy had a badly dislocated right elbow. The mother, in tears, said to the Resident, "I don't know why I do this, Doctor. When he cries and screams, I just hang him up in the closet. I never do it with his sister, just with him." (She herself, of course, had been physically and sexually abused as a child.)

The second 'case' (I have always not really liked that word) concerned two identical male twins, about 3 years of age. They were dubbed, in that cruel way that young doctors have of shielding themselves from the horrors of life by dark humor, the "Wolf Brothers." I was an Intern at the time.

The boys had been severely neglected, malnourished, and mistreated. They had no recognizable speech, but communicated only with one another, in a guttural tongue that only they understood. They were placed together in a single crib, where they both banged their heads against the wooden slats, and they screamed hysterically if they were separated, even for a few moments.

Some of your patients stay in your mind forever.

So I learned my craft, did well in it, and was enormously happy within it.

I had a reasonable number of boyfriends along the way, most of them in my own professional stream, and one quite serious love affair, which ended badly.

Upon completing my Pediatric Residency, I set about looking for a way to actualize my particular interests. I realized that a standard office practice would burn me out with boredom, as I was in fact something of an adrenaline junkie and drawn to the more urgent and dramatic aspects of Pediatrics. So I worked for a while in Emergency Rooms, but this denied me the continuous close contact with patients and families that I also sought. So then I worked for a bit in a series of Community Clinics, but this approach bounced me off the other wall of the lack of urgency and excitement.

A crux came a year ago, in 1981, when I applied for, and was accepted, for a more-or-less year's *locum tenens*, substituting for the permanent Pediatrician, at a Northern Ontario Indian Health Zone Hospital, located in a small town in the forest, called Sioux Lookout.

It was at Sioux Lookout, which served a huge, mostly roadless, area of forest and lakes, and which stretched from barely 60 miles north of the Canadian/US border to as far as the land went northwards, that I found the connection I was looking for. The tiny isolated Indian villages, mostly reachable only by float plane from Sioux Lookout, introduced me to working with people, especially children, of a culture and a world view, far different from my own, a culture in disarray and decline and under threat of extinction of its traditional way of life, and yet a culture that retained great intrinsic beauty and dignity.

Most of the children brought into the hospital by float airplane, or whom I went out to care for by the same means, were in relatively good nutritional condition; breast-feeding was universal in the isolated villages, which still depended on summer lake fishing by canoe and winter hunting and trapping by dogsled in the snow-covered forest and ice-locked lakes. However, for those families who had moved into the few towns and villages such as Sioux

Lookout or the larger Fort George along the US border, childhood nutrition was much less favorable; breast-feeding declined, poverty abounded, dental caries appeared with large intake of refined sugars, family disorganization, violence, and alcoholism increased, and suicide, including adolescent suicide, was not uncommon.

Knowing that these phenomena were not uncommon in what was then called the "developing world", I asked my friends and colleagues (hospital staff, the Mounties, the EuroCanadian schoolteachers) in Sioux Lookout what they thought was the 'solution' to these problems.

From this informal survey, my uncertainty was only compounded, when I realized that almost half the responses were: "It's just the way it goes, they will just eventually be absorbed and disappear into modern Canadian life", and almost the other half of the responses were: "The only way is to build a fence around it and keep them isolated from modern Canadian life."

During my months at Sioux Lookout, I also began to see connections between the life experiences, however different they might appear on the surface, of my mother's family in the Netherlands and that of vast numbers of people in the world of my own time.

Thus, as my time in Northern Ontario drew to a close, I decided that I might learn most about the former by living and working within the context of the latter. This was, for me, not so much a political calculus as it was a cultural and experiential one.

So, back in Toronto, I began to look for next steps that might give me the professional and personal satisfaction that I had found in Sioux Lookout.

Temporarily working again in an Emergency Room, my eye caught a notice in a medical journal placed by an organization called

'Canada Child Survival.' They were looking for medical staff to work in a famine relief setting in Ethiopia for periods of six-months or longer.

The combination of acute medical care of very sick children, the specificity of malnutrition, and (to be honest) the adrenaline adventure junkie-ness of Ethiopia, seemed to click everything into place. It would also be another way to postpone for a time, I confess, more definitive life-choices.

So I applied, was accepted, and, following a short orientation in Ottawa and then a month's brief course in "Tropical Medicine" in London, I find myself nearing the day to take the taxi to Heathrow Airport, and board, just after Christmas, 1982, a plane for Addis Ababa.

JAKE RILEY (DECEMBER, 1982)

I've been on plenty of airplane flights, but the one from Heathrow to Addis seemed to me a new departure, a door to a new life, and so in truth it proved to be. Africa!

We arrived about midnight, and as I crossed the tarmac and entered under the great dome of the airport, I realized that I was in a place unlike any I had ever been. Including Nam.

There were bustling crowds, mostly shiny black people, many of them lean-faced and very tall and straight, the men dressed in white robes, the women dressed in these long robes as well, with the frequent addition of white hoods. Others (Europeans? Ethiopians? 'Africans?') were in Western business or casual dress. There was a cacophony of voices calling, children squalling, unfamiliar sights, sounds, and odors, people rustling and gently pushing, no straight lines anywhere, but no sense of anything out of consensus or control. The few other European business or tourism travelers seemed as bewildered, and as fascinated, as I was.

What planet was I on? "Jake", I said to myself, "if only The Old Man could see you now!"

I collected my large rucksack and my old US Army duffle bag as it rolled towards me on the creaking revolving track, picked my way gently through the crowd (which, despite the aura of chaos, seemed to flow gently without bumps or inconvenience, or collision, sort of like goldfish in a crowded bowl of water), was waved smilingly through customs and immigration with only a glance at my passport, and emerged into a luminous night, warm and dry but with a cooling breeze, the lights of the city glimmering in the distance, moths and birds and bats swooping in tight circles, and "What Next?"

What Next proved to be a rickety taxicab, with a gesturing driver who seemed to be, like most everyone else I could see, afflicted with Smile Disease. I produced and handed him a note (written in Amharic, of which I could neither speak nor read a word), and a handful of strange currency; both items had been given me by the Canada Child Survival people in London, a world away. Smiley nodded vigorously, and we pulled bumpily off into the dark and winding streets, bound for Wherever Else. I was elated. My kind of evening.

Some ten minutes and, what, twenty thousand mileyears later, we pulled up in front of a shabby hotel, whose name could barely be made out under half-lit bulbs. No problem, because I couldn't read it anyway.

I pushed through the unlocked door, Smiley behind me with my gear. Across a small hall was the standard hotel desk counter with the pigeon holes behind it. Lying on the counter was the hotel clerk, snoring gently, bare toes occasionally twitching. Smiley Two professed himself (when gently shaken) delighted to see me (at least I think that's what he was saying), read my note upside down, made no attempt to find a mutual language with me, and proudly led me to my room, following his brief interchange with Smiley One, who saluted me grandly in farewell.

Within the hour of arrival at the airport, I was tucked up in a lumpy bed, in a small room, with the bed, a mosquito net, a washstand, towel, and bowl of cold water, a three-and-a-half legged chair, no closet, a dark window, and my baggage at my feet. "My kind of place," I mumbled happily to myself as I fell into a soft and dreamless sleep.

Starting the next morning, transition to my latest new life was comparatively simple. I followed my usual rules: "Be real good about Smiling Back; don't get bogged down in the details; don't sweat the small stuff; try to make yourself and everybody else comfortable; keep moving forward but don't force the pace; figure it out as you go along, but use what you have, learn what you have to learn, and then just do it. And look for Opportunity." Just the way The Old Man told me he had done it, when he himself had emerged upon a New World.

Getting hooked up with the nearby local Canada Child Survival office was easy, armed as I was with yet another indecipherable Amharic note. Learning to thread my way around at least my base area of Addis (nobody used the second word in the city's name) was no problem; there was always some street urchin who would be delighted to take me by the hand and, jabbering away, guide me, for a few of whatever the local pennies were called. This was also a very good way of learning to speak and understand a few words of Amharic—I worked very hard at this because I knew it was the key: the key to talking seriously and also joking with the Ethiopian porters and loaders and support staff and administrators at the CCS and at the truckyards and loading sheds that I would be driving in and out of; the key to being able to get myself fed and housed and pointed in the right direction in Addis and on the road; the key to picking up the necessary pointers from truckers and police and what-have-you in and around Addis; and, of course, the key to chatting up the local lovelies in the pubs.

I loved it. I loved the sky, the surrounding mountains, the sprawling dirty squalling smiling city, the laughing shoeless ragged kids, the grave self-possessed but helpful adults, the startling tastes and smells and sights and sounds. I loved it all.

If I had only brought my motorcycle, I would have thought I was in Heaven.

Of course, there was another side, a darker side, to it as well:

There were beggars in the shadows of the streets—blind, starving, hobbling on a wooden crutch, or sitting on a rag in the dirt, with an exposed leg that ended at the knee, or a face that had no nose on it. Ragged mothers holding out reedy bundles of babies with pus in their eyes, young boys leading blind men, each holding one end of the same long stick. Scrambled markets with flies everywhere on the produce, where you had to be sure that you and your wallet were still together. Clumps of refugees from the wars and famines in the provinces; looking as lost as they made you feel upon seeing them. Police and soldiers, heavily armed, lots of them, pushing through the crowds, barking rather than speaking, leaving silence in their wake. People seemed to keep some magic distance, about a foot and a half, away from them as they moved through the crowds.

Despite my somewhat privileged upbringing, I had always thought of myself as a working-class guy, by trade and by temperament, but I had never seen nor conceived of poverty of this degree, even in Nam, except maybe in some of the burned-out villages, and I was un-nerved by it.

Sometimes, in the hustling, bustling, chattering market, it would suddenly, without warning, go absolutely silent. Sometimes this would be preceded by a shout, or a sharp cry, but mostly it would just happen, out of nowhere. Then, there would be a flood of movement, of sound, sometimes gunshots, sometimes not, and people would scatter like crows driven up from the cornfield, to get away, anywhere, to get away.

All was not well, in Addis. And, as I was to learn, elsewhere in Ethiopia.

With the help of CCS, I soon found myself a small apartment, on a quiet narrow alley off a busy street. Downstairs from me were a couple of American Peace Corps Volunteers, teaching English in what passed for a local school. Their (the PCV's) Amharic was quite good. I made a deal with them: I would cook them a terrific dinner once a week, if they would speak to me only in Amharic, except when things collapsed completely. This worked quite well, and we had some good times together; it was, of course, the ideal way for me to learn and polish my Amharic. Pretty soon I was able, with lots of bumps and lumps, to take care of myself in the market, on the road, and as I went about my work.

Canada Child Survival had a small office, and a large transport and storage yard, not far from my apartment. Their principal activities were two: to provide staff, including where possible medical staff, to the two major famine relief centers that they collaborated with in Ethiopia, and to transport food relief, medical supplies, construction and whatever other materials were needed, to those centers. To my delight, they assigned to me a huge French Berliot truck, all mine, which didn't go very fast, but did go almost anywhere and over or through anything. This pleased me immensely, especially since I was expected to be able to handle my own maintenance and repair, to be able to fix whatever needed fixing as I traveled long distances over bad roads in lonesome country. Just my thing. I spent more time rolled out in my bedroll, under my truck and the Ethiopian stars, than I did in my apartment.

I got along well with the Canadian and other expat CCS staff, and especially well with the Ethiopian staff, who were hard and serious workers, but always ready with a smile and a laugh and a couple of elbows in each other's ribs at my atrocious Amharic. I threw myself into my work, and of course, into my play.

CCS, and the trucking activities that supported it, were involved in two major relief sites in Ethiopia; they were quite different sites in all respects.

The first was about 175 kilometers from Addis, to the south, and along mostly paved, and pretty fair, roads. It was within 20 kilometers of a town called Hosaina. The site had been chosen partly because it was a central point for refugees on the move, but particularly because adjacent to the relief camp was an existing small mission hospital.

Founded in 1969 by the Ethiopian Catholic Church, and heavily supported by an Italian charitable foundation, Saint Luke Hospital consisted of a group of cement block and mud-brick, metal- or thatch-roofed buildings, with running water and semi-reliable electricity. It was staffed by 5 nuns: an American nun who was also a physician, and nursing sisters from the Philippines, Italy, Ireland, and Ethiopia. They were supported by one medical- and a number of nursing- assistants from the Ethiopian Public Health College at Gondar, local support staff, and frequent 'guest' short-term volunteer physicians in various specialties from Europe (Italy in particular) and North America.

The original plan for St. Luke, a plan they had been making good progress on before the current political chaos and famine, was, in addition to developing and expanding the usual hospital services, to develop outreach preventive, clinical, and environmental health services for the small villages dotted around the area. But now their progress was severely stalled by the ever-expanding flood of famine refugees that flocked into, and through, the area, most of them in desperate circumstances and many in great medical, surgical, and obstetrical need. Particularly urgent were the small children with acute severe malnutrition and accompanying infectious illnesses. Saint Luke hospital was drowning.

I would make one, or sometimes two, round-trips a week between the CCS yard and Saint Luke, hauling medical and surgical equipment and supplies, food relief, large amounts of intravenous and oral rehydration fluids, and construction and support materials of all kinds. The trip would take me about three or four hours each way, and with the loading and unloading, and whatever other kinds of assistance I could provide to the Sisters, I would usually stay over-night at the hospital or relief camp, rolled out in my bag under or alongside my truck. The roads weren't half-bad, and in this area were generally safe from marauding bandits or soldiers. I usually drove the route alone, in radio contact with CCS in Addis.

The second CCS site was another story entirely. It was located almost 600 kilometers from Addis, off to the east, beyond Dire Dawa and the ancient city of Harar, and about 20 kilometers southeast of Jijiga. This was close to the Somali border, and Djibouti and Eritrea were not far to the north. The closer you got to the area, the more barren and harsh the landscape got, and the more severe the effects of the famine appeared. This part of the world had been a battle-ground between Ethiopians, Somalis, Eritreans, bandits, Christians, Muslims and whomever else (including most recently the Italians) for many centuries, and continued to be a hotbed of dispute and terror; in my view this is highly likely to continue for a long time, and perhaps forever, with only changes in the actors and the weapons used, not the circumstances.

The Jijiga Relief Camp had no hospital in proximity; Doctors Without Borders had a small operation connected to the camp, where they did their heroic and extraordinary work.

It was a full day's drive from Addis, and sometimes longer, for me to reach Jijiga, and was, in truth, dangerous driving, sort of like being back in Nam, but without the ground and air cover. CCS would always send two trucks in convoy, with an assistant driver accompanying the regular driver in each truck. Radio contact was not always reliable, help was far away, and the risk of banditry or worse was real. Opinion varied as to whether it was better for the drivers to be armed, or not.

I would haul to Jijiga about once every 10 days or 2 weeks, and it was at least a three day round trip. Because of my skills and experience, I was usually the senior driver, and in the lead truck. We never traveled alone, and never were on the road after dark or before daylight.

On my third or fourth trip on the Jijiga run, I was in the lead truck as usual, with a cheerful assistant driver from Morocco, from whom I was trying to learn a bit of French of the most useful variety. Behind us, in the second truck, were two Ethiopian drivers.

As we rounded a sharp bend in the road, there they were, spread out across the road in front of us: a semi-circle of armed men, about ten of them, aged from adulthood down to pre-teens, and clad in a variety of cammo and cast-offs. Most were armed with old bolt-action rifles, and a few had AK-47's. No one was smiling.

I slammed on the brakes, and hand-signaled the second truck to do the same. I twisted the volume knob all the way up with the radio in 'Receive' position, but did not try to transmit.

My Moroccan buddy reached onto the shelf behind the driver seats for the 12-gauge shotgun lying there; I shoved his hands aside and motioned to him to put the shotgun away and out of sight under the seats. There was no way we were going to be able to shoot our way through, and the best course by far was to avoid a gunfight in which we were completely out-numbered and out-gunned.

The bandit leader, a nasty-looking piece of work with a burn scar where his right ear and cheek should have been, stepped up to my door, tossing his head in a clear signal for me to get down from the truck.

Instead, I rolled down my window, and said, "Speak English, Buddy?"

The guy tossed his head again with a scowl, so I continued, in a mixture of English, broken Amharic, and a bit of Italian, trying to explain that we were delivering food and medicine to the refugee relief camp on down the road. This at least slowed the guy down, so I offered him a cigarette; the whole pack was accepted. Then I offered him a swig of water from the bottle I kept under the seat. But, whatever, I was not getting down out of that truck.

There was some back and forth, which eventually led to smiles and even laughter, mostly conveyed in more-or-less universal gestures, rather than words. And then the bandits stepped aside and let the trucks pass.

But not before relieving me, and the other drivers, of whatever cash, in whatever currencies, and whatever jewelry and wristwatches, we had on us.

From that day forward, I have never allowed a weapon to be carried in any truck I drive.

ELSA (DECEMBER, 1982)

I was quite groggy by the time my plane landed in Addis around midnight; I had gone straight from a final session at the London School of Tropical Medicine and Hygiene to my apartment to pick up my baggage, then an endless taxi through the traffic to Heathrow for my early evening flight, then only restless snatches of sleep on the plane, and there I was. No problem getting through the entry formalities; I hardly noticed the whirl of activity and the totally unfamiliar scenes of the arrival area. All I wanted was sleep.

As I passed through immigration and customs, a tall, slender Ethiopian man held up a sign: "Welcome, Dr. Lisa." I realized that had to be me, and that particular mistake was one I was more than familiar with through the years, so I walked directly to him.

The driver took my luggage from the khaki-clothed porter who had snagged it from the revolving ramp, gave him a tip, and he guided me out into a warm night with a cool breeze, a zillion stars blazing the sky.

Into the CCS-logo'd 4-wheeler, straight down through the dim lights of the city, and through the doors of a run-down-looking hotel. The night clerk was asleep, his toes twitching occasionally, lying flat on the desk counter. My driver reached over the clerk, who snored briefly, and lifted a room key from the pigeon holes. Without disturbing the clerk, he guided me to my simple but comfortable room, bid me good night in faultless English, and I was off to Dreamland. Airport landing to bed in less than an hour.

What seemed only seconds later, but was actually 6 hours, I dressed, ate a simple breakfast (great coffee!), and the same driver whisked me off to spend a few hours with the friendly but overworked CCS staff, and then once again I was back in the same vehicle and driven 3 hours down to the Saint Luke hospital.

The road down became progressively lumpy and bumpy in direct proportion to our distance out of Addis, and similarly the traffic got progressively more sparse: ragged cars, taxis, smoke-belching buses, donkey- and horse-carts disappearing in favor of massively-overloaded trucks and a few similarly-overloaded long-distance buses.

The hospital was nearby to a small town, really more a village than a town. As with all the small towns we had passed through, the one-road through was crowded with small shops, street vendors, darting children, donkey and horse carts, a few battered vehicles here and there. And people, horses, donkeys, dogs, a few chickens, and ubiquitous urchins selling single cigarettes—all bustling in the main street. Back off the main street were a few adjoining dirt roads lined by wooden shacks.

If we had passed through the larger town of Hosaina, I never saw it. In fact, in the busy months to come at Saint Luke, I never did get to see Hosaina. Or perhaps I did, and just did not recognize the metropolis.

A quarter-mile from town, Saint Luke Hospital appeared to be simultaneously being building-up and being torn-down. The main buildings were of well-constructed concrete, with sheet-metal roofs. Adjacent to them were bungalow-style ward buildings, some of concrete blocks, some of mud brick, some with metal roofs and some with thatch. There was a separate operating and delivery block, and a rudimentary clinical laboratory. A tiny separate block contained, I came to learn, a huge wooden crate, which itself contained an x-ray unit—neither unpacked nor assembled, and unusable until the required level of electric power could be supplied, sometime in the indefinite future.

The wards themselves were mostly open to the air, with wide doors and narrow window spaces. Shady verandas lay along the lines of the wards, and clotheslines for drying sheets and ward linens ran along the back. A short distance away was a colony of smaller bungalows, for the staff, with several common dining areas and a separate building for a kitchen. The ward area had its own central kitchen, hand laundry, and several outbuildings. The hospital complex had basic electricity, supplied from a shed containing a diesel generator, but available only several hours a day. There was running water, piped from a well, in the hospital complex, but only sporadically available in the wards themselves.

About 200 yards further on from the hospital complex lay the tents of the refugee relief camp. Originally, it had been hoped to have individual tents for small family groups, but this plan had proved impossible to carry out, given the increasing pressure of numbers. Some attempt at orderly 'streets' and groupings was still attempted, but increasingly the camp became a hodge-podge of tents of various sizes, types, and locations. A number of latrine enclosures and ditches had been dug a short distance from the tent encampment, but many, if not most, of the camp's residents just went off a short distance into the surrounding bush. Between the tent housing and the hospital proper there were several medical tents—one for waiting patients, one for examination and treatment, and one serving as a holding- or short-stay ward (all ages, both sexes, and all conditions) for those patients who, for one reason or another, were not accommodated in the hospital proper.

Numbers of residents in the camp fluctuated by the day, indeed by the hour, but were somewhere in the range of many hundreds, not counting those who were just 'passing through' but needed medical attention. Water for the camp itself was drawn from hand-pumped wells, and there was no electricity. What lighting there was had to come from either battery-powered flashlights or kerosene lanterns.

Deposited at the main entrance to Saint Luke Hospital, I had barely gathered my luggage from the van when Sister Marlene, the hospital 'manager' came bounding out the door to greet and forcefully embrace me.

"Dear Dr. Elsa, I am so glad and so grateful that you are here," she said. "We are overwhelmed, especially with regard to the children, and we have never had a proper Pediatrician, save for short-term visiting doctors. Come, have a cup of tea, and let's get acquainted and plan out how things are going to work."

Sister Marlene was actually Doctor Sister Marlene Murray, an African-American Board-certified Obstetrician-Gynecologist from Philadelphia. She had been sent to Saint Luke as a member of the Missionary Medical Sisters. Short, wide, bursting with energy and good-heartedness, somewhere between forty and ageless, she was tireless in her work, unfailingly positive in her outlook, and with a short fuse for anyone who was not the same. If there was a crisis: medical, surgical, or administrative, or personal, she was the person you wanted to have at your side. If there was no crisis, she would look around and try to discover, or create, one.

In short order, Sister Marlene and I talked over a plan of action (actually, the good Sister did most of the talking and planning, but listened intently and took into consideration all of my ideas).

Sister Marlene had already caused a small personal tent to be set up for me to live in (My first personal dwelling, prior ones being only our Toronto apartment and a variety of rooms in dormitories or staff quarters!). Upon pushing back the tent flap, I discovered it already 'furnished' with a folding cot, a few stacked wooden boxes for holding clothes and possessions, a camp chair, small table, wash-basin, canvas bucket for drawing water, and a kerosene lantern and various flashlights. All the comforts of home!

Nearby was another new tent, for the examination of arriving children, and adjoining it, a third separate tent to serve as a pediatric ward for children who were not better housed in the regular hospital wards.

Sister Marlene had assigned to me one or two Nursing Assistants to work with me, and one Ethiopian Clinical Officer, a recent graduate from the Gondar College of Public Health; he was able to perform primary care functions independently under light supervision. What laboratory work that could be done would be done at the main hospital lab. I would be directly responsible for the new 'Pediatric Unit', on call 24 hours daily, seven days a week, and also for seeing pediatric new arrivals and outpatients at a morning and afternoon clinic.

At my suggestion, Sister Marlene agreed to try and find resources and staff to create some sort of 'feeding station for nutritional rehabilitation' for the many incoming children with acute malnutrition (starvation, really) as they arrived at the relief camp, but for the moment I would just have to make do with the set-up as previously described. I had not considered, until Sister Marlene brought it up, that all the children would be accompanied by their mothers, who would sleep in the tent wards with them, alongside in or under the crib or bed, or together on the floor, as the case might be. I began to think about how I might use the mothers themselves for a resource of hospital care.

In addition to all the above, of course, I would need to be available 24/7 to cover any pediatric emergencies that occurred in the hospital labor and delivery rooms.

"So that's it, My Dear," said Sister Marlene. "We can add more and smooth off the edges as we go. Now let me take you round for a quick hello to the other staff, then you can put your stuff in your tent, meet us for dinner, and then you can get going. Righty-Oh!"

My head was spinning, and not just from fatigue. The reality suddenly struck me that, much as I had thought of myself as having experience at Sioux Lookout and in hospital clinics and emergency rooms, I was now in a totally new environment, which would combine large (? overwhelming) numbers of desperately-ill children, at all hours of the day and night, day in and day out, with only inadequate knowledge, inadequate resources, and inadequate staffing to see myself though. And, most probably, not much ability, or time, to communicate verbally with my small patients and their parents.

And there was nobody on the other end of the non-existent telephone Help Line, be it 3 in the afternoon, or 3 in the morning. "Welcome to Ethiopia, Elsa. It's what you asked for."

By the time Sister Marlene and I had finished our 'Planning Session', it was time for dinner. The food was simple, a combination of Ethiopian and semi-Western, and delicious. In addition to Sister Marlene, the other 4 nuns who were nurses were welcoming, and a lively conversation was carried on in English, Italian, a bit of French, and Amharic (which I resolved I had better get to work on immediately).

There was also a 'visiting doctor', Dr. Sergio Gennari, an Italian general surgeon, who turned out to be a demon for lightning-fast work, tireless, committed to doing as much as possible in the shortest possible time, and possessed of great humanity and a biting, sarcastic sense of humor.

The final member of the 'staff' dining table was the Clinical Officer, Asfaw Desta (Ethiopians usually employ two names, the first being a given name, and the second a patronymic. So—Asfaw, son of Desta). Tall, lean-muscled in that Ethiopian way, he was a young man in his early Twenties, quiet and reserved but with a twinkle in his eye, and clearly a favorite with the rest of the staff. Asfaw's English was excellent, with an American accent. I instinctively felt that I could trust him.

As dinner ended, and I nodded off for the third or fourth time, my head dipping towards my plate, Sister Marlene suggested that, since there was such an enormous amount of work to be done in the morning, getting me organized, in addition to beginning to deal with the existing pediatric patients, and seeing the new patients, who would begin to arrive about 7 a.m., it would be a good idea for me to get to bed 'a bit early'.

Easier said than done. I tossed on my cot, trying to get my thoughts in order, thinking of what I had, what I could do with it, and what I didn't have, and what I couldn't do with it anyway. Eventually, I fell into a fitful sleep, and had a dream so transparent and yet so profound. In the dream, I was standing upright. A huge dark wave, turning upon itself, rumbling, rising to even darker skies, raced towards me. As it came forward, it grew larger and larger, higher and higher. And I myself grew smaller and smaller.

I woke, drenched in sweat. To calm myself, I decided to categorize what I actually had in terms of my past experience and resources:

--A high-quality medical education, but one based on a wealth of technical resources, ample personnel for teaching, training, and immediate consultative support or referral.

--Several years of experience with patients, most of whom spoke my language, and most of whom presented with complaints and illnesses that were caused by disease processes which my training had specifically prepared me for.

---a manageable schedule (though very heavy by conventional standards), with easy access to more-experienced physicians, a well-stocked medical library and access to medical journals.

I thought back to two sayings traditional among medical students and young physicians:

"Common Things are Common." "When you hear hoofbeats in the street, look out the window and expect to see horses, not zebras."

Well, what if the common things were not things I had ever had experience with, or even knowledge of, before? And what if they were alligators and elephants, rather than horses or even zebras?

And who could I turn to for advice? Or consolation? And, what if, as seemed certain, the alligators, elephants, zebras, and even horses came in floods and armies, and not one at a time.

And then I thought about my mother, Christina, cycling out to 'The Farms', searching for food in the Hunger Winter. It became clear to me that what I needed now was what Christina had needed then: Determination. Courage. No-nonsense. Just do it.

So I decided that I would. I rolled over and went back to sleep.

In the morning, I awoke at five, and took stock of my tangible personal resources. In a shoulder carry bag, I had brought onto the airplane: Nelson's Textbook of Pediatrics (the North American classic); a well-recommended South African Textbook of Pediatrics and Child Health, which I had not yet read; the Harriet Lane Handbook—a small yet dense compendium of tables, formulae, lists, and organizing principles.

Most comforting of all, I had with me my precious 'Mechanical Brain'. Medical students and young physicians almost universally carried such a movable and expanding feast, usually in the form of a pocket-busting black six- or eight-ringed notebook. The Mechanical Brain was an instrument in which one could record all sorts of useful practical information: percentages of this and that, names and doses of important medications, methods for calculating surface areas, miniature height and weight nomograms for growth of young children, mnemonic tricks for remembering such things as the sequence of the Cranial Nerves ("On Old Olympus's Towering Tops, A Finn and German Viewed Some Hops"), normal patterns of the various electrocardiographic leads, etc., etc., etc. (I still have mine, and will keep it forever, unless someone invents some sort of electronic pocket-size computer.) The Mechanical Brain made you smarter than you really were, and all in your hip or lab coat pocket. It was invaluable for recording 'Pearls' (in medical student parlance, a 'Pearl' is a pithy saying or factoid or concise bit of information, usually conveyed by a Senior Physician, which condenses important knowledge into a small but shining bit).

In my carry-on roll-aboard, I had packed my pen-light flash, my Littman pediatric stethoscope, and my Welch-Allen otoscope/ophthalmoscope with varying-size ear pieces. And, of course, I had my always-present multi-bladed Swiss Army Knife, in a small, beaded, chew-softened leather sheath hand crafted in Sioux Lookout by a third-trimester Ojibway lady, flown in to the hospital from her village to await labor and delivery.

That was it. Now I had to go about seeing what I could do with it, and how fast, and for low long without rest.

So, fortified, I rolled over and got forty more winks.

Promptly at 7 a.m., Asfaw scratched on the tent flap. Already there were more than 35 children, with their mothers, lined up outside the Exam Tent. For this, my first day, Asfaw was going to stay right alongside me, rather than each of us seeing our own stream of patients. Two Nursing Assistants were at hand to help move things along. Patients had to be examined, treated or prescribed for , sent to the hospital tent or ward for admission (for later further examination, treatment, etc.), or sent away ('home' did not seem like the appropriate word, these patients being sent back into the Relief Camp, or, many of them , moving on out, with their families, into the bush towards who-knows-where). The most sketchy of notes would accompany them in any case.

Suddenly, I looked up and realized it was well past noon. There was no one left in line. Asfaw, wiping his brow, told me that we had seen 'only' 90 patients. Of these, we had admitted 5 to hospital, since, as Asfaw said," We didn't see too many very sick kids this morning."

I attempted, only partially successfully, to remember exactly what Asfaw and I and the Nursing Assistants had done in the preceding 5 hours. What I DID realize was what a God-Send Asfaw was: smooth, steady, calm, and efficient. And he did not frighten small children, unlike the strange lady with the white skin and yellow hair, who seemed to not understand a word of what their mothers said.

I had had no breakfast, which was to become a habit. Asfaw and I took 15 minutes after clinic to grab a cup of coffee (and use the toilet) in the staff area, along with whatever else was left over from lunch. Then we had to push on to attend to the 5 new admissions, make quick rounds on the 20 or so children who were already on the ward, perform any required procedures on those patients, interrupted by the dozen or so 'new' outpatients who just turned up during the afternoon, four of whom required admission, including one tiny baby, perhaps ten days old and born 'on the road', wracked by the convulsions of neonatal tetanus (which I had never seen before); the child expired within an hour of admission.

Then we were through for the day, except of course for a quick set of Evening Rounds, to button up the two wards (tent and main hospital). Part of those rounds were done just before, and just after, a quickly-swallowed dinner. Asfaw did not seem to indicate that the day had been anything unusual, though he did say that it was fortunate that we had not been called to the Delivery Room for a problem of neonatal resuscitation or other untoward event.

I slept well that night. No dreams. Up again at sunrise. That would be the pattern, on an 'easy' day. On most days, there would be either a larger number of complex or critically-ill outpatients (requiring more ward time and procedures to get sorted out), or urgent problems with the existing ward patients, or hours spent with a difficult problem in the Delivery Room (which required in turn more time spent in the ward, if successful), or a greater number of outpatients turning up, or, or, or...

Asfaw and I worked smoothly together. Generally, we each took a separate stream of outpatients, one of the Nursing Assistants staying with me to translate. If we could, we got as much as possible of the inpatient Morning Rounds done before starting Outpatient Clinic. We tried to do inpatient rounds as much together as possible, or at least have a look at the most critical patients together before splitting up to do diagnostic or treatment procedures, but this was not always possible. There were many things I could teach Asfaw, but actually there were many more things that he taught me (diseases that I had no experience with, ways to safely cut corners, etc). Evening Rounds we always did together (unless one of us was trapped with an emergency on the ward, on arrival, or in the Delivery Room), and tried to get everything under some semblance of control at the 'end 'of the day. Sometimes there was no 'end of the day' because of a middle-of-the-night major problem.

By the end of the first ten days, I felt I had a partial, if slippery, grip on things. Most of the time, anyway. I was chronically fatigued, but it seemed as if it had always been that way. Sometimes I was proud, feeling as if now, at last, I was a 'Real Doctor'. Sometimes I was full of grief, tortured by a sense of incompetence, ignorance, and inadequacy. And, sometimes, often, in fact, I was terrified: of that call in the night, of that unexpected event on the ward in the morning, of that next patient in line, carried dead in her mother's arms.

Often I thought of a favorite quotation, written by a young Russian doctor in a cottage hospital deep in the forest in 1918, later published in a book by him entitled "A Country Doctor's Notebook." Mikhial Bulgakov wrote what I now knew to be true: "Sometimes you will do the wrong thing, and no-one will ever know. And sometimes you will do the right thing, and no-one will ever know."

JAKE (FEBRUARY, 1983)

Well, I was on the now-familiar 'Milk Run' down to Saint Luke's that Monday afternoon, hauling powdered enriched skim milk, intravenous fluids, and medications, for what I had heard was the new 'Child Health and Pediatrics' area of the hospital. For the past couple of weeks, I had been hauling heavy construction loads to both Saint Luke and Jijiga, and I hadn't had a chance to see what was going on, nor to meet the new Pediatrician.

I pulled up alongside a tent I hadn't seen before, with a hand-written sign on it: 'Children's Outpatients and Examinations.' As I did so, the tent flap opened, and out stepped an unlikely duo.

The Ethiopian boy looked to be about 5 or 6 years old. Shoeless, wearing only a ragged pair of shorts, he was sobbing. He was holding tightly to the left hand of a woman, and from my partly-sideways view, the boy had a strange golf-ball lump about mid-way down along his spine.

The woman had a few tears of her own in her blue eyes. Her left hand held the boy's right hand, and in her own right hand she was gripping a small, ragged, Teddy Bear.

She was, to my appraising eye, Caucasian, of average height, slender, and dressed in not-very-tidy green scrubs, covered by a long, and equally-untidy lab coat. In her right coat pocket was a coiled stethoscope, and in her left pocket was a black ring notebook, a ball-point pen stuck between the rings. On her feet were well-worn running shoes. On her head was a blue and red Toronto Blue Jays baseball cap, and from under the cap poked strings of straw-colored hair.

Now I am not by any means a 'Thunderbolt Stricken' type of guy. But at this moment I was, well, Thunderbolt Stricken.

I really don't, honest, remember exactly what I said, or if I said anything. But I must have, or I think I did. Or something.

Could it really be I really said, or thought, "Excuse me, Nurse, I was looking for, I mean, do you know where I could find the new Pediatrician?"

No, now really, this is me, Jake, but I must have said something, because the woman just gaped at me, maybe just like I was gaping at her. But that's ridiculous.

And then, she laughed. Not very loudly, but she laughed.

And said something like, as best I can remember:

"Well, whatever that's about, we can talk about it some other time. Right now I have to get Robel here up to see Dr. Gennari, and see if he would agree to take a crack at this tuberculous spinal abscess, if I can first get Robel on TB Triple Therapy first, for a couple of weeks. Potts Disease, you know, never seen it before. His mother (Robel's, not Gennari's) has just now died of Tb; she's inside the tent. So, if you'll excuse me....it's been nice to meet you..."

I was confused, incredulous, non-plussed, and embarrassed beyond belief (and these are not words that are commonly applied to me). But something else, too. Something like a puppy looking at a Rubik's Cube.

So I just got back up in the truck, moved it a hundred yards down the line, and began unloading supplies, as I had been instructed back in Addis, near the tent. I covered them carefully with a tarp, which wasn't totally necessary, since it had not rained in ten months. Then I got back in the trunk and drove, Hell for Leather, back to Addis.

ELSA (FEBRUARY-MARCH, 1983)

It hadn't taken me very long to figure out what 'common things are common' meant in my present situation. In fact, it was pretty straightforward: what it was really about at Saint Luke was starvation. Starvation of chronically-malnourished small children. Children who most all had common pneumonias (which I had had plenty of experience with in Canada), or common diarrhea (ditto), but complicating an underlying protein and/or calorie malnutrition: the combination carrying them off in great numbers.

Alternatively, there were the children who had other serious diseases (the worst example being measles, in an environment where measles vaccine was not available), and who had previously been balanced on a nutritional knife-edge, and they would 'recover' from their measles, but fall, several weeks later, into a severe state of malnutrition, which, often, they did not survive.

It really didn't matter, when you came right down to it, whether you considered that they had died of 'infection', or died of 'malnutrition'. The underlying cause, in both instances, was starvation.

Whether the children who came to that tent in the morning were longer-term residents of the Relief Camp, or whether they were with families that were just passing through, fleeing the drought and the political chaos, coming from who knows where and going to who knows where: the critical element facing my pediatric practice was starvation. And the therapy of starvation was...food. Just like my mother had learned, 'Going to the Farms', those long years ago, in the Hunger Winter.

But for me, now, here: what food? How procured? How prepared? How delivered? How to make up for the dwindling breast milk of exhausted (and themselves starving) mothers? What foods could be obtained and provided for infants and toddlers whose parents had no cash, no remaining agricultural resources, few surviving (and themselves starving) cattle, and no settled and safe place to live?

I dug in and read all I could, in Nelson (not a lot of direct help for my situation), the South African text (better, much better) and whatever books I could find or borrow from others at the hospital. I learned about marasmus (the Biafran Babies from the Nigerian Civil War—acute caloric starvation in young children, usually, but not always, early in the second year of life). And kwashiorkor (from a *Ga* tribal word meaning "the child displaced from the breast by the next-coming child"), a mixed protein and calorie malnutrition, often precipitated by acute infection, usually diarrhea or pneumonia), and about the various vitamin and mineral deficiencies. I was a quick learner, mostly between late evening and dawn, when reading and thinking replaced sleep. Asfaw and the nuns and the nursing assistants had very useful practical knowledge to import, and with the availability of powdered milk substitutes and supplemental iron and vitamins and other childhood food supplements, all furnished from CCS, I felt myself beginning to acquire a bit of traction.

But I knew that this was all temporary and only partially successful. What was needed was to avoid the starvation in the first place. And this was impossible in my situation, as it stemmed both from factors of environment (drought), and factors of society (poverty, war, and political chaos). A far-second best 'solution' would be to find a self-sustaining 'permanent' basis for adequate nutrition; this might not be impossible, but would be extremely difficult, and I pondered, especially during those long night hours, how we might achieve some small approach to this, especially for those refugee families who were on the move.

JAKE (LATE FEBRUARY, 1983)

Look, you know me; I am usually one to forget about my mistakes and just move on, though I am never hesitant to apologize when I am in the wrong (seldom though that may be). But even I was aghast as I thought about what my behavior had been (or might have been, as confused as I was about the situation) on first sight of Dr. Elsa (which, I learned, is what everyone called her).

So I fiddled with the schedule a bit, and managed to avoid the Saint Luke route for a couple or three weeks, sending down one of the other truckers, and having myself assigned to the longer and tougher Jijiga haul. I said to myself, only half-kidding, "bandits are less to be feared than making a complete ass of yourself."

And yet, and yet....the image of those blue eyes stayed with me. I hadn't seen many blue eyes in a while. And that Toronto Blue Jays baseball cap! In Ethiopia! I was a Kansas City Royals guy myself, but it had been a long time since I had seen any baseball, let alone played any.

So I steeled myself, picked up a load designated for Saint Luke, and headed on down. "In for a dime, in for a dollar", as The Old Man used to say.

I timed it so as to arrive in the late afternoon, figuring I might be able to catch Dr. Elsa in between her clinics and dinner. As it turned out, she was actually in that three-minutes 'free' space following the final outpatients of the day. As I jumped down from the truck, I could see Asfaw Desta going ahead to start Close-Out Rounds in the in-patient tent, probably on the children they had admitted to the hospital that day.

I had to scurry to keep up with her as she headed from the Outpatient tent up towards the hospital ward area. Her stride was actually a bit longer than mine, and she showed no sign of slowing down. In fact, I wasn't even sure of any sense of recognition on her part.

Hustling forward to keep pace, my head turned to face her, Old Careful Jake stumbled on a stone and fell to the ground. So there I lay, looking up at her as she looked down at me (she had deigned to halt to render whatever emergency medical aid might be necessary).

From my less-than-impressive position, I sputtered out a few inadequate words of apology, not at all the ones I had carefully rehearsed in the truck cab coming down from Addis.

Surprisingly, she took off her Toronto Blue Jays cap, scratched her head, and said something like: "Look, don't worry about it. It just happened, like a lot of strange things around here, that's all. Don't give it a second thought. Look, I'm really, really busy right now, up to my eyeballs. Look, come by again some time, and we'll have a cup of coffee and introduce ourselves in a more appropriate manner. Look, it's OK. OK?"

And, as Dr. Elsa pushed on, I knew a brush-off when I (infrequently) encountered one.

Actually (Dear Diary, if I was really keeping one), it wasn't as simple as that. When Elsa and I got to know each other (much) better, she confessed that she had smiled to herself as she left me behind in the dust. And after that first disastrous meeting, if you could call it that, she had asked Sister Marlene about the CCS driver, leaving out all the details. Sister Marlene replied that she didn't know him very well, but he was always very polite, and always stayed to help store the loads he brought down, and to help with anything else he could that needed doing. And, of course, that usually meant staying for dinner with the staff, and then he usually just rolled out in his sleeping bag alongside his truck, and was gone by morning. She told Elsa that she would 'introduce them' the next time I came down; "It would be nice, Dear, for you to get to know another Canadian, I mean, American."

Very impressive. Jake Riley, Boy Scout.

ELSA (MARCH, 1983)

I began to figure it out. The basic principles of anatomy, physiology, and pathology are the same, wherever you are. The approach to patients: taking a history (it helps if you speak their language), physical examination, deciding what the problem is, or might likely be (called 'differential diagnosis'), performing whatever lab or imaging tests to reach or support a diagnosis, and then undertaking whatever medical or surgical therapeutic measures as appropriate: these are standard under most any circumstances, in most any environment. "All" that I had to do was to learn, and become familiar with, whatever specific diseases or injuries occurred in Ethiopia (many of them things that I was already well-prepared for, but also very many of them things that I had no or little prior knowledge or experience of), and then proceed as I was trained to, but much more rapidly, and with no time to dawdle. On the one hand, the diagnosis and treatment of a fractured humerus caused by an automobile accident on the TransCanada highway was technically little different from that caused by a kick from a donkey in the village market.

The rub, of course, was two-fold. At Saint Luke I was very often encountering conditions about which I knew next to nothing, and about which I had to learn the specifics from which to make a diagnosis and provide adequate treatment: malaria, neonatal tetanus, acute polio, various parasitic infestations, far-advanced and dissem-inated tuberculosis, and so forth.

Some things were in concept much the same in Ethiopia as in Toronto: diarrhea, pneumonia, meningitis, septic joints, celluli-tis, obstructed labor and premature infants, blood stream infections, traumatic injuries, etc., though more frequent and usually far-more advanced upon presentation.

And then there were those things that I had seen a great deal of in Toronto, but of which I encountered very little, or none, in Ethiopia: asthma, diabetes, nephrotic syndrome, and a much lesser prevalence of sore throats, middle ear and urinary tract infections--- were they truly less prevalent, or was I just missing them, my rea-soning crowded out by other confusions? What would account for these differences? Environment? Human Behavior? Horses crowded out by Zebras?

Working out these lines of thought, gave me, perhaps para-doxically, some confidence: that I could do my job by applying what I already knew, learning what I did not know, and then applying that approach step-by-step, improving as I went. Journey of a Thousand Miles…sort of thing.

Fortunately, the hospital was quite well stocked with most of the medicines that I needed, with the very major omissions of ade-quate laboratory facilities, a modern blood bank, and an x-ray unit. But I was privileged to have an excellent surgeon (for as long as Dr. Gennari was there, or when a replacement arrived). Sister Marlene was a highly-competent obstetrician/gynecologist, the nursing care was devoted and of high quality (including one of the Sisters being a nurse-anesthetist). And then, of course, there was Asfaw.

Asfaw was a treasure: to Saint Luke and to me, not only for his language and cultural awareness, not only for his quiet and unselfish devotion to patients, not only for his significant knowledge and experience, but also for his technical ingenuity and practical skills. I had always thought myself pretty good in that latter department, but many of Asfaw's abilities were far beyond mine. He was a master at threading needles into the smallest scalp- or hand-veins, for drawing blood or infusing fluids; he rarely missed a clean spinal tap on first attempt, even in a screaming, struggling infant. When it came to doing 'cut-downs- of the lesser saphenous or external jugular vein to provide a more permanent portal of access to IV fluids, or relieving a tension pneumothorax (yes, the occasional adult battle casualty would wander, or be carried, into the hospital), he was almost better than Dr. Gennari. In fact, when the surgeon needed an assistant for a particularly complicated procedure, he would often call on Asfaw (that, of course, would play havoc with my own day). One could see in the young Ethiopian the makings of a truly great physician.

As I struggled to work out for myself a conceptual framework that would allow me to be as effective and efficient as I could be, I put into the equation those things that were major handicaps or barriers:

First, of course, was my profound ignorance of where I was, who my patients were, and what the important parameters of their lives consisted of. Language was the key, and I struggled mightily to learn the basics of a functional Amharic (which still left me in complete ignorance of patients whose language was not Amharic, but one of the many other, often obscure, tribal languages in Ethiopia). Even with good translation, and the Nursing Assistants were invaluable here, mysteries not easily solved abounded regarding the cultures, beliefs, and life-settings of my patients and their families.

Another fundamental dilemma was one related to my own medical training: in North America, medical students are taught to attempt to find a single, unified diagnosis that combines as many as possible of the various symptoms and findings that the patient presents. But, in places such as Ethiopia, virtually all patients, especially pediatric patients, are suffering from multiple, often not-closely-related, diseases simultaneously. So searching for a unifying diagnosis not only does not help, but actually can mislead: the malnourished infant who enters with severe diarrhea also has chronic malaria, intestinal parasites, and iron-deficiency anemia. Also, perhaps the child has an infected burn from an overturned pot on the fire. I learned that I had to think in multiple directions at once, instead of in a linear fashion, and to do that under great time pressure, pressure that was unrelenting, and did not allow for adequate physical, mental, or emotional recuperation.

I often thought of my situation as representing a modified hourglass, filled with sand. But there was a hole in the top of the hourglass (where my increasing knowledge, skills, and relevant experience would be poured back in), and a hole in the bottom of the hourglass (where my fatigue and, yes, despair at the unremitting pace and extent of the pressures upon me, both physical and emotional, would leak out). Depending on the situation of the given day, or night, I was not often certain whether the balance of the sand was positive or negative.

JAKE (LATE MARCH, 1983)

Well, as The Old Man used to say, "If it won't fit, don't force it; get a Bigger Hammer." I decided that I could make a better start with Dr. Elsa if we had a 'second' meeting (the first two, clearly, were so bad that they only counted for one-half each, so what most people would have thought of as our third meeting was, to me, really only to be the second encounter). Never say die, Jake, keep moving forward.

I left Addis as early as I could, and got to the hospital about noon, determined, as I said, to make a better start between us. My excuse would be that I was carrying a large load of medicines, supplies, and equipment for the Pediatric Service (indeed I was; I may sometimes fib, but I never lie), and needed for Dr. Elsa to show me how and where to put things.

It worked (perhaps, I think now, by mutual if unspoken consent). I figured that, rather than fumble around with complicated apologies, maybe it would be better to just start off afresh. Perhaps Elsa (enough of the "Dr." bit) had the same thought; in any case we found it absolutely easy to get over the preliminaries of who was from Toronto, and who from Topeka (and where that was), etc.

Later on, when things had taken their much better natural turn, Elsa told me that, as we were sorting out the stockage and storage of the material I had brought down from CCS, that she was surprised at the keen eye that I had for putting the right things in the right place, for the most efficient access and use. And that, in fact, I had made a couple of suggestions regarding the arrangement of the tents and the receiving lines that had her wondering why she had not thought of them herself. And she said that she appreciated the way I asked questions without assuming to know the answers, and put my own suggestions without pushing them onto her.

That got me to telling her about The Old Man, and about his Gift, and how I dearly hoped, and only half-believed, that I had inherited some of it myself.

So that got her telling me about her mother, and what it took for her to be 'Going to the Farms' at age 12, and how she hoped that when the chips were down that she, Elsa, could have the same courage and determination.

So, to make a long story short(er), we figured out how my Dad, Jacob, and her mother and grandmother, Christina and Freddi, had been pretty much in the same place at the same time in May of 1945. And how, if things hadn't turned out exactly the way they had for each of them, that we would not have been standing here in Hosaina, Ethiopia, in 1983, talking about it. We were both quiet for a while after that.

Elsa invited me (by this time we knew that we were missing lunch) to have a look inside the children's ward tent. We entered the semi-gloom (the problems in a large tent, assuming it does not leak, are insufficient light, and inadequate circulating air, especially in hot climates).

What happened next was so very important to everything that happened after that that I wrote it all down, in as much detail as I could remember, as soon as I got up into my truck, headed back for Addis. I think I got the quotes pretty exactly, or as close as makes no difference. Much later, I asked Elsa to fill in the blanks.

So here is what happened, and what was said, from Elsa's point of view:

"As we entered the tent, I felt Jake stiffen, and take a deep breath. At first I thought it was the spectacle of so many kids, so sick, in a few cribs, several children in one cot, mothers lying on the tent floor under the cots or beside them, nursing their babies. What was 'the usual' for me, I assumed was a shock to Jake."

"But Jake moved directly to a far corner of the tent. Propped up in that corner, her back against the tent wall, was a string bean of a girl, about 10 years old, holding out an empty glass. Her left leg was bent under her, creating a sort of lap for herself. But her right leg was extended almost straight out, flaccid, and obviously she could neither move it, stand, nor walk. I of course knew that the child was a recent case of polio; there was nothing to be done; she would remain with a non-functioning right leg for life."

"Jake went directly over to the girl, took the empty glass from her hand, filled it from the water jug near the tent door, and returned and placed it in her outstretched hand. As she smiled up at him (I had never seen her smile before), he bent over her, and I was amazed to hear him begin to murmur softly and reassuringly to her---in rapid Amharic! The girl, who I knew had been virtually mute, withdrawn in her immobility during the week she had been in hospital, broke into a shy smile, and actually said something in reply. How had he done that? What was it, something about Jake and females? Surely, more than that."

"Jake came back over to me as if nothing had happened. I just looked at him: 'in wonder' is the only way to describe it. " Jake, how did you do that?"

"Well (Elsa said I replied), my father, Jacob Riley, his right leg, the war in Europe, you know… Yes, you know, as she eats more and gets a little stronger, I'm sure I could rig something up, a metal and leather kind of brace that fits her, and maybe it could be modified as she gets bigger, why not? And, yes, maybe some kind of what do you call them, Canadian crutches, with the little things for the forearms to steady them, and, you know, I'm sure I could work something up. I'm pretty much a good tinkerer, runs in the family. You should have seen my Grandfather, The Old Man. Well, anyway."

Now it was Elsa's turn to be speechless. She told me, much later, in Addis, that she had known that that had been 'The Moment'.

But what she did say, after a moment, without regaining her composure, was: "Jake, you could make it so she could walk again, couldn't you! And my grandfather's name was Jacob, but I never knew him. He was lost, during the War, in Europe. Where they were all so hungry. Until your father Jacob. Until the airplanes came, with food. My mother told me all about it, she was the one who had to go search for food. She was twelve years old."

Funny how things work, isn't it. After that, there was plenty to talk about. By the time I left to go back to Addis, there were all sorts of plans about when we could talk some more, what I could do to add on and improve things at the hospital, and so on and so forth.

But that wasn't really what it was all about, was it. Of course not.

ELSA (MARCH, 1983)

Of course I knew the famous Dutch story about the boy who stuck his finger in to plug the hole in the leaking dike, staying alone all night in the darkness after discovering the leak, and saving the village from a flood.

There I was, but the night was endless, and there was, in truth, no way to plug the leak.

The drought worsened, the political chaos increased, the flow of refugees multiplied. And, especially of concern to me, the number of children and the severity of their starvation and illnesses increased.

There were, by late March, almost a thousand refugees in the Relief Camp. The United Nations and voluntary relief agencies such as CCS were strained to their limits to keep up with the situation in the camps in Ethiopia. More people in the camp meant more, and sicker, patients at Saint Luke. More refugees on the road (what roads?) meant more patients 'dropping in', more patients in the hospital, longer lines at the Outpatient Clinics. Asfaw and I would see two hundred or more children each day, every day, and were unable to admit to hospital all those who needed it. We trained several of the Nursing Assistants to handle more and more of the 'routine' outpatient load, but how do you really define 'routine' when you are in a desperate triage environment, and more patients than you can handle aren't really 'routine' at all. Asfaw and I developed a simplified and not-really-adequate system of triage, of doing what we could with what we had, knowing that there really was no way of staying ahead of the curve. By March, we had been forced to set up a second tent for outpatients, so now we had more than fifty inpatients as a constant census, and would soon need another tent as well.

Just because there is a war and a famine on doesn't mean that 'ordinary' people don't get sick in 'ordinary' ways as well, some quite serious or life-threatening. So in addition to the long lines at the outpatients, and the pressures on the hospital beds that stemmed from the war and famine, there were, of course, what would have been the 'normal' patient loads of better times.

I asked myself, "How do two doctors and several nurses and assistants care for 200 outpatients (none with trivial complaints) and 50 inpatients every day? I know what the answer was: 'Not adequately.' I thought about how small was my little corner of Ethiopia , and how many millions of refugees from hunger and chaos there were. But the bulwark to maintain sanity, as my mother and grandmother had learned, left no alternative but to just put your head down against the wind and to , as Jake would put it: 'Keep Moving Forward.'

In addition to the greater numbers, the children were more desperately ill, largely because their nutritional status was worse than formerly. The hospital could provide relatively-effective nutritional rehabilitation, and Asfaw and I developed a program helping mothers to themselves produce appropriate foods from the supplements provided, or from what they themselves had, or could garner on the road. This activity required yet another new tent, and the training and assignment of yet another Nursing Assistant from the hospital to work, full-time, with the mothers.

But all this was never enough, could never be enough. The Children of the Drought came to Saint Luke more seriously malnourished than ever, with or without the diarrhea, pneumonia, or other infections. One precipitated the other. More children died shortly after admission, some even died while waiting in the receiving lines. More surely died after they were discharged, often discharged prematurely to make room for others, who died in their turn. Depending on how you counted it, the death rate of children admitted to the pediatric ward was about twenty percent.

And that was not counting those children whose families by-passed the hospital, or could not reach it in time.

I tried, using 'professional distance' or mental tricks, to keep this from wearing me down, but it wore on me, how it wore on me.

One of the things that I found most painful, as I have said previously, was the considerable number of children who died in line while waiting to be seen, or died very shortly after being admitted to hospital. Pondering about this one night during the midnight hours, I was reminded of my friend Scotty.

Scotty was from somewhere in the Caribbean, of indeterminate but at least middle-age, and was a very smart lady with virtually no formal nor medical or nursing training. She was, in fact, an Orderly in the Emergency Room at Toronto Children's, something that she had been doing for many years. As mothers and children would come into the ER, they would register at the desk, and then go and sit on the long benches, often for long periods of waiting, until they were called to see one of the four or five doctors who were examining patients individually in eight or ten small rooms.

Scotty had developed the extraordinarily useful capacity to differentiate, by just keeping her eyes open, the not-very sick child from the dangerously-ill one. This, by the way, is one of the most valuable skills in pediatrics. She would roam ceaselessly around the waiting area, and if she saw a child that needed immediate attention, she would go over to one of the doctors and quietly suggest that it might be very good to 'take a look at this one' right away. The doctors, myself included during my training years, learned, at their peril, not to ignore Scotty's gentle hints, especially in the wee hours of the night, which was when she was usually on duty.

Smiling to myself, I rolled over and drifted off to sleep.

The next day, I watched the Nursing Assistants working with Asfaw and myself, and then had a talk with Sister Marlene. Identifying the most likely candidate, we gave that young woman the primary job of roving up and down the long lines during morning and afternoon clinic, picking out those infants and children who were most at hazard, and moving them immediately up to the head of the line. There, she would observe and assist Asfaw or myself as we examined the child and provided emergency intervention as necessary. The Nursing Assistant's 'Scotty Sense' increased very rapidly. No data was kept, but I had the clear sense of two things: One, the Nursing Assistant's 'pre-training' skill was much greater than we had given her credit for, and Two, many deaths were averted by this measure (or, as the cynic would say, at least postponed).

JAKE (APRIL, 1983)

Saint Luke was growing, well, not really growing, more like expanding, and changing rapidly, with challenges and stresses in all direction. I had, and have today, great admiration for the character and competence, and devotion, of the hospital staff, starting with Sister Marlene and right on down to the sweepers. And as to Elsa, I tried to look past my growing personal feelings for her, and see the extraordinary professional she was. But, for Elsa, as for everyone else at Saint Luke, the pressures of caring for the ever-increasing numbers of patients were tremendous, and challenged mind, body, and spirit in ways that I had only seen more difficult in Nam.

I tried to do my part; with each visit I made, bringing down supplies, I tried to find ways of making myself useful, not only as push-pull-lift, but using my technical and mechanical construction skills, my organizational and planning bent, and what I got from The Old Man about being cheerful and optimistic and going 'straight at it' even on the darkest days. I began to spend more and more time at Saint Luke (and yes, of course I had an ulterior motive), more frequent trips down, almost always staying overnight, sleeping bag rolled out beside my truck (and usually near the you-guessed-it tent). Often I would spend several hours the next morning, working on things at the hospital before high-tailing it back to Addis. The

CCS management cut me a lot of slack, because they could see some value in my modest accomplishments. Elsa and I saw a lot of each other, but it was mostly on the fly, and we had very limited personal time together.

And then, just like The Old Man said Opportunity did, along came "The Great X-Ray Event", which, I blush to say, led to Sister Marlene calling me "The Hero of Saint Luke."

One day, I asked Sister M, "What is in that enormous wooden crate; that one in that area over by the Labs and Pharmacy? She replied that it was a packaged x-ray unit, donated by an Italian charity, but that nobody at the hospital had known how to set it up, and, most importantly, how to deal with the problem of the hospital's inadequate electrical system.

"Hmm…I got on my 'Thinking Look', and said, "Maybe I could have a look at it, see if perhaps something might be done. Next time I come down…"

So I went to work on the problem, or, rather, on the Opportunity, and, to make a long story short: a few false starts and some truly dangerous and spectacular tinkering with the hospital's (and the town's) electrical system, the x-ray unit came on line, though it was usable only for a couple of hours each morning.

The addition of the X-ray to the hospital's capabilities was amazing. Sister Marlene's and Dr. Gennari's diagnostic capabilities moved further into the Twentieth Century, not to mention Elsa's and Asfaw's. At first the physicians had to take and develop their own films, but soon yet another Nursing Assistant was in training to partially take over those tasks. In addition to the reality impact, it was a tremendous morale boost for people who were working their hearts out.

Sister Marlene insisted on a celebratory dinner in honor of Yours Truly, at which Elsa and I spent most of the time smiling at each other; many humorous stories were related by the guests (quite a few at my expense), and a number of bottles of good Italian wine from Dr. Gennari's private stock were consumed.

After the dinner, Elsa and I found ourselves walking out into the surrounding bush, quiet under the luminous stars of the dazzling Ethiopian sky.

After a long time, Elsa said (how could I forget her exact words?): "You know, Jake, in some strange way you give me courage to go on, and to do better, much better than perhaps I know how to do. Sometimes, here, I feel as if I am drowning, not so much from the load, but because I know that I can't really make any difference in the longer run. It just keeps coming, and I can fix it here or there or for one or another, but then there is just another child, another mother, with either the same or a different thing, over and over and over again."

"So, Jake, when I saw you with that polio girl, automatically lighting up with ideas to make her life truly better, and now, turning that old crate of boards into an x-ray machine that will forever transform this hospital, I think: 'Maybe I can do that too. Maybe I can, not just keep plugging along, but actually learn to fly. Maybe I can be magic, like Jake'. Somehow you convince me of that possibility, and give me strength."

I was quiet for a while, thinking, and then replied, "I feel it is the other way around, Elsa. I watch you, the beautiful you in the Toronto Blue Jays baseball cap, staying with it, day after day, having the determination and the strength to take whatever comes through that tent flap, never slowing down, never bending back, never saying

'Wait a minute, give me just a minute, just, just, let me back off, let me give up, just this once.'

"For me, Elsa, on the other hand, it's easy. It's just the way I'm made, the way my parents, and especially my grandfather Matthew made me. I see something that could work better, or different, and 'Pop', my wheels begin to turn. I don't really have a choice. If it's broke, I just fix it. If it ain't broke, I just fix it better anyway. If I can make it go faster, or further, or work better, my Jakeness just turns on to it. Autopilot. No credit due. Next problem. So I watch you, and I think, 'maybe I could have true courage, the courage to hold fast, to keep on going while knowing the demand is never going to stop. Like Elsa.' "

We walked a little further, and then turned back towards the tent and the truck parked beside it. I took Elsa's hand. Elsa, for just a moment, laid her head on my shoulder. No words were spoken.

Then Elsa, on her tent camp bed, and me, rolled into my sleeping bag alongside my truck, fell smoothly into sleep. I know what my dreams were. I wondered what were Elsa's.

JAKE (MAY-JUNE, 1983)

When I awoke next morning, Elsa was already on her way down to the Outpatient Tent. I called to her, me half in and half out of my sleeping bag, and as she turned and looked back at me, I realized that, once again, I had no idea at all of what to say to her. There I was, in my skivvies, hair askew, mouth catching flies, wide opened, and just nothing at all came out.

Elsa took two steps towards me, and she also seemed incapable of thought or speech. So, I kid you not, this is what she did: she took her Toronto Blue Jays baseball cap off her head, swung her arm around, and bowed deeply and graciously, and said—nothing.

For my part, I stood straight and tall in my tangled sleeping bag, and gave my best formal military salute.

Some days later, we agreed, the deal was set, right there and then. Once and for all.

I had plenty of time to think about it, driving back to Addis. Elsa, I would guess, not so much, as she plowed into and through the morning's work.

For me, it was a difficult concept. But what it boiled down to, was that I knew, in a way I didn't know how I knew, and could not describe, that after all the wheels and speeds, and after Alaska,

Montana, California and Wherever Else, after Nam, and England and Western Europe (and some quasi-legal jaunts into Eastern Europe), and Addis, and Hosaina, and Jijiga: after all those miles, I was home.

For Elsa, she told me later, it was somewhat the opposite. She felt as if she had been catapulted, or rather catapulted herself, into a new world, if not a new universe. For months now, she had been focused on looking DOWN, down at the endless lines of the unknowable, the unthinkable, and the unbearable. Months of near-constant inadequacy and doubtful outcomes, of persistent fatigue, worry, and sorrow. It must have been like that for her mother, Christina, during the Occupation, she thought. All of a sudden now, she was looking UP, up to where everything seemed to be possible, just because it was. She was liberated.

So, I was gathered in; Elsa was flung out. Both of us were transformed.

So, of course, my trips down to Saint Luke became, if anything, more frequent and prolonged. There was plenty of work to do, to say the least, for both of us, and our pattern became that in the late evening we would walk together, out into the surrounding bush, under the explosively-brilliant Ethiopian sky, walk for what seemed like miles, and then sit and talk, and touch and hold each other. There weren't many large logs or large rocks to sit on, but around the hospital there were plenty of discarded cement blocks, pieces of timber, etc., and I, as usual, tinkered up a somewhat comfortable 'sofa-without-cushions' out of the debris, set it out some distance from the hospital and the tents, and it became, as they say, 'our place' in the evenings.

In the meantime, life, as distinct from what Elsa and I considered our life together, went on pretty much as before.

ELSA (JUNE, 1983)

It was coming on to six months at Saint Luke for me; my contract with CCS had stipulated 'six months or longer.' Even had not Elsa and Jake gone a long way towards becoming ElsaandJake, I would have decided to stay on throughout the year, doing the best I could and also, of course, giving Sister Marlene and the Missionary Sisters of Philadelphia or CCS time to find a replacement Pediatrician. When I discussed this with Sister Marlene, the nun told me how gratified and humbled she was at my determination and accomplishments, how sorry all of Saint Luke would be when I left, how glad they would be if I could stay 'forever', and how she hoped that a new Pediatrician could be found to arrive in, say, November, so that Veteran Elsa could break in the 'Newbie.'

Sister Marlene was well aware, as of course was everyone at Saint Luke of 'what was going on' between Jake and me. With a half-smile, she said, "Well, I can guess Jake will be leaving at about the same time, no? He will also be very hard to replace, Dear Man that he is."

"Well, we haven't discussed that", I replied. "But (with a smile and a wink) that might be so." And Sister Marlene actually giggled in response, "Back to work, eh, Sweetie."

About a week later, near noon, I was elbows-deep in diarrhea, pneumonia, and malnutrition, with a side dish of meningitis, when an aide from the hospital ran down to the Outpatients with the message that Dr. Elsa was to immediately turn everything over to Asfaw and run straight up to the Delivery Room, where there was a neonatal emergency.

When I arrived, and started scrubbing up before I caught my breath, Sister Marlene, already at the operating table, filled me in without taking her eyes from her own work.

A woman, who had only arrived at the Relief Camp the previous night, in late pregnancy, had gone into labor around three in the morning. The Nursing Sister who was attending her soon became aware that labor was not proceeding normally, and at about seven a.m., when the fetal heartbeat began to slow down, alerted Sister Marlene.

The baby was in breech position, labor was completely obstructed, there was a partial placenta praevia (the placenta overlapping the birth canal with a real risk of intra-partum hemorrhage), and the increasing fetal and maternal distress provided clear indications for an emergency Caesarian Section. So Sister Marlene's job was to get the baby out while preserving the mother's life, and my job was to make sure the baby survived.

A Nursing Assistant provided drip anesthesia. Sister Marlene was already beginning to enter the abdomen as I finished scrubbing, gloved up, and began to look around to see what I had available, and to think through what I could do with it. There was a competent Nursing Assistant, who had laid out the necessary drugs and equipment, an oxygen tank with a flow tube and a tiny face mask already attached, but no neonatal Ambu squeeze bag or other positive pressure airway device. A pediatric laryngoscope with a newborn-sized blade, a number 3 endotracheal tube for intubation, and an array of syringes, needles, and appropriate medications for neonatal resuscitation were neatly laid out on a side tray. A bassinet lay to the side of the operating table, and a couple of small blankets had already been warmed and were waiting. Now all we were lacking was a living, breathing baby.

"Good job, Esther," I said to the Nursing Assistant, as I turned to see how Sister Marlene was proceeding. What I saw was Sister Marlene extracting the baby, held head down by both heels, from the open uterus, quickly cutting and clamping the cord, with the baby lower than the mother's body, and handing it across to me, while she turned to getting out the placenta and, hopefully, avoiding a maternal hemorrhage.

I found I had hold of a baby: apparently full term and of good size, blue-black, not crying, not having taken a first breath, limp, and with a slow but detectable heartbeat. No sign of pink on the palms or soles.

I had been here before, but also knew that each one of these incidents feel like the very first one: uncertain of outcome, and with time definitely not on your side.

Quickly, I flicked my fingers against the soles of the baby (a boy, I noted). No reaction. I instructed the Nursing Assistant to turn the oxygen flow on gently, and hold the mask over the baby's face loosely. No reaction.

After checking that the baby's nose and mouth were free of mucus or other debris, I picked up the laryngoscope and trach tube and gently, but firmly, used the scope , while gently pulling the baby's jaw forward and opening its mouth, to visualize the baby's epiglottis and tracheal aperture, and inserting into it the endotracheal tube (this is probably the most demanding and difficult manual task in the Pediatrician's armamentarium, especially under the stress of a child on that knife-edge between living and dying). As rock-steady as I could get, 'thinking not-thinking', I performed a smooth and successful intubation, which had not always been my prior experience. I smiled to myself as I recalled the old medical school aphorism: "See on. Do one. Teach one."

"Super-Dooper," said Sister Marlene, not turning her head from her work of neatly closing the abdomen. But we were not out of the woods yet, not by a long-shot.

With the baby tubed, I instructed the Nursing Assistant to hold the flowing oxygen mask loosely over the open end of the trach tube. No reaction. Heartbeat present but slow, well less than 80 beats per minute. Muscle tone poor. Color poor. No attempt at spontaneous respiration.

I grabbed the oxygen mask and kept the flow going, while instructing the Nursing Assistant to bring the standing goose-neck lamp closer to keep the baby warm. I began external cardiac massage. No reaction.

"Esther, draw up 1 milliliter of epinephrine, one part in ten thousand solution, that is ONE PART in TEN, repeat TEN thousand. Give it to me in a small syringe with no needle attached, NOW, and prepare a second dose of the same in reserve. Be sure NOT to use the one part per thousand standard epinephrine solution.

I took the plastic syringe and squirted the epinephrine (adrenaline) solution forcefully into the endotracheal tube, down to the lungs, where it could be rapidly absorbed, into the bloodstream, into the heart, as a stimulant. No reaction.

Two minutes later. Out of time now. Last chance. "Do it now, Elsa, Just DO IT", I told myself, not realizing I was shouting. "Esther. Give me that second syringe, 1 ml of one TEN thousand solution. NOW!

Down into the endotracheal tube again.

Time stood still for a long, long moment. Then the dawn came up: heart rate increased, color turned pinkish-chocolate, soles and palms pink, and a strong, angry cry emerged as the baby decided that, yes, he would enter this sorry world after all. Respirations began, became steady, and the baby reached his tiny arms out, fingers outstretched, fingertips curling into tiny fists as he grasped and held onto his life-to-be.

Sister Marlene and I looked at each other, held each other's gaze for a moment, in that secret mutuality that only Pediatricians and Obstetricians know. Sister Marlene was already almost finished closing and cleaning up (now I understood why the secret name that the other nuns used for Marlene, but never to her face, was 'Sister Flash'). The mother was lightening up from her anesthesia; there had been no significant hemorrhage. Clearly, things were going to be fine on the maternal side.

A half-hour later, Sister Marlene and I found ourselves together in the ward, watching a tired and sleepy but contented mother, baby nestled beside her and making sucking noises.

It doesn't get any better than that. Ever. Sister Marlene reached out her two hands and grasped mine. Holding each other, arms outstretched, she and I began to dance around the ward. When a few of the other ward patients began to sing softly in Amharic, Marlene and I danced faster, in rhythm with each other, our patients, and the cosmos.

JAKE (JULY, 1983)

As July came near (and my Yankee Doodle Birthday), I thought the time was about ripe for me to take another step in what I thought of, sort of, as 'My Elsa Plan'. Her mood was much brighter following the successful delivery of the baby, who, by the way, had been christened by his parents, with the wisdom of people who live close to the world around them, Marel. I would have preferred Elmar, but Elsa said that sounded too much like Elmer Fudd, which would make no sense in Ethiopia.

So I approached Sister Marlene first, explaining to her that I was concerned about the unremitting strain on Elsa, physically, and psychologically, now more than six months straight 24/7, with no relief. Sister Marlene nodded, knowing, without doubt, what was coming.

"Well," I said, "I was thinking that if she could have just a couple of days off sometime, I , you know, could take her to Addis with me, she could see the sights, we could take it easy, and, you see, she would come back refreshed and more relaxed."

Sister Marlene nodded again. "I think you are right, Jake, and, Ahem, how good it is of you to think so carefully about Elsa's welfare. No time like the present, and may you both be very happy together…

How about this weekend? Asfaw is increasing daily in his high competence, and being 'in charge' for a bit will only increase his self-confidence and maturity. You know, 'See One, Do One, Teach One.' I can send one of the Nursing Sisters and an additional Nursing Assistant down for extra help, we can stretch and cover it, and, besides we have to get used to the future absence of Elsa, even though I have high hopes for Philadelphia or CCS finding us a replacement, both soonest for Elsa, and next year for Dr.Gennari."

Elsa herself at first expressed some reluctance; after all, she had two kids in the ward with neonatal tetanus, a bunch on the severe malnutrition re-feeding regime, a really worrisome infant with pneumonia, and a couple of diagnostic dilemmas, plus a lot of and-so-far and-so-forth, as usual. But I convinced her (it really wasn't difficult) that none of that was other than the constant and the usual, and that a break would do her good, and even increase her ability to keep rolling until the end of the year.

So Elsa threw her stuff together (basically clean jeans, T-shirts, and undies, the Toronto Blue Jays baseball cap, and a comb and toothbrush) and, within hours, she was headed north, having her first ride in the Berliot truck, which she promptly christened 'Jake's Jag'.

Elsa was now past the days when anything could terrify her; her experience of facing down life and death, and her insights that she said she had gained from me (!), had taken her well past that. But she was, I know, at least a tiny bit, well, terrified. Both she and I knew that we would make love, sleep together. While I doubted that she was really a virgin, it was clear that she had not had a great deal of experience with men. She had told me about a few boyfriends in University, her one meaningful and severely painful love affair during medical school, and not much time for anything else during her then-traditional routine of 36 hours on/12 hours off during much of her Internship and Residency training, and hardly anyone her age or eligible while she was at Sioux Lookout. I realized that for her this weekend was going to contain a lot of unknown territory. So I was, myself, a little bit terrified as well. Elsa took the edge off it right away by musing that it might not be totally dis-similar to going out to beg, borrow, or steal food from the Farms, when you were twelve years old, and that both of us were a good deal further along than that.

I think, on the ride to Addis, Elsa was a little bit gathered into herself. On the other hand, it was now my turn to be flung out into the universe, my thoughts providing me pictures of a limitless, time-less, future.

Turn about is fair play. Yang and Yin.

In the event, it was not surprising. Elsa was passionate, Jake was patient. Jake was passionate, Elsa was patient. What more can I say?

My little apartment was perfect, if just a trifle untidy. When I confessed that my birthday was right about now, we invited the Peace Corps kids from downstairs for a hilarious and magnificent, if I say so myself, dinner, cooked by Yours Truly (Elsa hardly knew how to boil water, and that mostly for sterilizing instruments). This time, most of the humor was directed at Elsa, instead of at me. The Doctor was blushing.

We wandered around Addis, but not too much, because we spent so much time inside the apartment. Elsa made a very brief visit to CCS, to talk over details regarding her staying at Saint Luke through December, and the need to recruit her replacement. I intro-duced her to my best buddies in the trucker community. We browsed a bit in the colorful markets. But mostly it was about being together, so closely together, going further and further and deeper and deeper along the now conjoined trails of our lives.

Two days passed too quickly. Actually, it was three days, two in Addis and one half-day each way on the road. On the way back to Saint Luke, I drove as slowly as possible.

As we drove out of Addis, Elsa said, "Jake, when are you taking off for Mombasa? If you are going to get to Asia before the end of the year, aren't you cutting it pretty close?"

I replied, "Well, Ellie (where that word came from I didn't know, and her brief frown made sure I never used it again), I've been thinking. As long as you decided to stay through December, I thought maybe I would continue with CCS, as is, until then, or at least until then, or something. They can easily find a replacement for me (maybe not as good as I am, but anyway a replacement) on short notice. Actually, I've talked to them already about staying on through the end of the year. And then, in January, maybe we could, well, I mean, you know, sort of, we could well… we could see. That's it, we could see."

"Ah, yes, Jake, that sounds like one of your really good firm plans, your usual brilliant articulation and foresight. Yes, good plan. Stop the truck!"

And when I did, almost before I came to a complete stop, Elsa threw her arms around me and kissed me until my eyes crossed.

And so we arrived back at Saint Luke, with everything settled and mutually understood.

A week or so later, after telling Elsa that my next trip down I would have a surprise for her, I turned up at Saint Luke with a package of my own devising. One part of it was a pair of two sleeping bags, with long zippers so that they could be joined into a single wide (not too wide) bag. The other part was a single camp bed, fashioned by putting two beds together, without the two slats that held one side of each bed getting too much in the way of them being placed alongside each other. I called the package, 'The Riley Tinker's Solution.'

Elsa gave me that look of hers that I know signifies, 'Oh, Lord, what will come out of that brain next?' But she was smiling while she did it.

So I said, "Well, you see how that could work. In the usual good weather, we could sleep out (I really like to sleep out, like both my Dad and Grandpa did) next to my truck. Or, if we wanted to, we could sleep on one big special camp bed in the tent. Or, if it got cooler, or if it ever rains again (which I don't think is going to happen, but it might), we could bring the doubled bags into the tent and cover ourselves in the double camp bed. Neat, Eh! (I had taken up from Elsa the Canadian use of the ubiquitous expression, 'Eh!'. I found that it gave me a tiny extra bit of time to think when I wasn't completely sure of where I was going next).

It took no time at all for everybody at Saint Luke to get used to the new arrangement. Some wag (probably actually Asfaw, though it might have been Sister Marlene) hung a sign on the tent that said, "Elsa and Jake."

ELSA (LATE AUGUST, 1983)

As I remember, and how could I forget, it was just before seven a.m. four weeks ago, and already the day's dry heat was gathering in a cloudless, rainless, blazing sky. Dry, cracked, sandy, loose, rocky— whatever the land base was, wherever it was, the foliage was scarce, stunted, blighted. And the land was waterless.

The refugees coming in to the camp, and the sick coming to the hospital, continued to grow in numbers: poorer, sicker, more emaciated. But I had a sense that the increase in the proportion of children, especially infants, carried along with the families, was not keeping pace with the increase in the proportion of adults. Perhaps, I thought, this means that more children are dying along the route, or that less children have been conceived. Or both.

A small group of the Saint Luke staff, who had been talking together before the start of the long day's work, was just breaking up. Sister Marlene was off to scrub up for a hysterectomy. I was on my way down, a few minutes behind Asfaw, to start the morning out-patient clinic. Jake was kidding around with Dr. Gennari in mixed Italian/English. Jake himself was getting ready to drive back up to Addis, and had given me a hug and a peck on the cheek in fare-well (everyone was used to this by now, and everyone approved, especially Sister Marlene). Shadowing Jake was a small boy of about 7 years old, from the Relief Camp, who followed Jake around all day, every day that Jake was at Saint Luke, mimicking his every move and gesture from four small steps behind him. Jake liked to pretend he wasn't aware of this, but also liked to slip the kid a piece of candy from Addis from time to time, which kept the cycle going, to their mutual pleasure. Several of the Nursing Assistants were chatting, in the usual multiple Ethiopian tribal languages.

Suddenly, a soldier from the town, in a ragged uniform (a member of the troops stationed in the area at this time of chaos and lawlessness), burst onto the scene, shouting irrationally about "Italians" and "foreigners" and "spies." Waving his semi-automatic pistol, he fired 3 shots into the group, and a fourth shot under his own chin, blowing his head off.

The first round hit the small boy full in the face, killing him instantly, and showering blood and brain matter all over Jake.

The second round took Dr. Gennari's right thumb and forefinger off at the wrist, depositing them in shreds several feet away, and ending his surgical career.

The third round missed everyone, and went wherever missed shots go.

For a few moments there was stunned silence, then shouting and screaming. I turned and dashed at Jake, incoherent in my fear, convinced that he had been hit. When, rubbing the gore off his face with his sleeve, he assured himself and me that he was unharmed, I regained composure, and immediately pulled from my lab coat pocket the short length of rubber tubing that I carried with me (always), grabbed Dr. Gennari by the right arm, and tied a tight tourniquet around his right wrist, dragging him up to the hospital while

I held his right hand as high above his heart as possible, so that Sister Marlene could clamp and tie off the severed blood vessels, suture what was left of the most valuable part of his body, and stop the flow before he bled out from his radial artery.

After that, everyone just stood immobile and silent for a few moments, trying to comprehend what had happened, which was obvious, and why, which was unfathomable.

Then Jake climbed up in his truck and headed back for Addis, I turned and went to start seeing patients in the line, and everyone just got back to coping with the endless, endless routine.

For some days afterwards, the hospital lived in a miasma of grief and disbelief. Sister Marlene placed three small candles in a sheltered niche near the main entrance to the hospital. When I asked her what they were for, Sister Marlene replied, "The first is for Lost Innocence, the second is for Punishment, and the third is for Forgiveness. " The candles were left to burn down to lumps of greyish wax.

Dr. Gennari, the icon of indefatigable energy for work, and razor-sharp wit, mixed with loving-kindness for all humanity, was evacuated back to Italy. Word reached us at Saint Luke that, upon returning to his hometown of Orta San Julio, beside the lake, he refused the idea of reconstructive surgery for the remnant of his right hand, and, after a week or so 'at home', disappeared completely, not to be seen or heard from again. Sister Marlene added a fourth candle, next to the remains of the other three, and when asked what it represented, said, "Recognition."

JAKE (LATE SEPTEMBER, 1983)

The disaster of the killings seemed to mark a subtle but irreversible shift in the context of Saint Luke itself. The gap left by Dr. Gennari's loss was as much psychological as physical (the absence of a surgeon, especially one as talented and untiring as Dr. Gennari, was a heavy, heavy blow to the daily functions of patient care). Sister Marlene was run ragged. Nursing Sisters and Assistants had to step up to duties they had not assumed before. Asfaw came into his own as a senior partner, able to rush from pediatric care, to adult medicine, to surgery. Elsa gave him a new and fitting nickname: 'Hermes.'

But the surgical output of the hospital, never equal to the need, fell further and further behind, as, inescapably, so did staff morale. Elsa was pushed almost beyond endurance, and perhaps further, without the full-time help and partnership of Asfaw.

Without Sister Marlene's towering leadership (though she was, indeed short and somewhat stout), things might have actually come unglued, with the very real consequences of less people helped, and more people not surviving. The patient load and the Relief Camp population continued to increase, and there were more and more-severely malnourished adults and children among that population.

Elsa expressed the question of whether Ethiopia itself was completely disintegrating, and whether Saint Luke might disintegrate with it, adding its own small weight to a massive social collapse.

She and I were talking about this one evening, as we sat on the 'cushionless sofa' at the rim of the endless bush. Far to the west, enormous waves of heat lightning (dry, no rain), flashing in green, white, and yellow curtains between earth and sky, seemed to display an air bombardment of destruction on a towering scale. Elsa, seeming to probe the very depths of her own exhaustion and despair, asked me how it would all end.

"Well, it will all end, sometime and some way," I replied. "Rain will come, eventually, and perhaps even the outside world will wake up and make a real effort here, eventually. But the 'eventually' is quite certainly pretty far away, and so our job here is not really to 'do good' but rather to do what we can to minimize the bad. Every kid you pull through, every family that survives intact, will add to that tiny bit of 'better' to the mix when it becomes possible to make a new start. You and I will be long gone, and the ones that replace us will probably also be long gone, but that's really all we can work and hope for. And, of course, put your chips on Asfaw."

I thought a bit for awhile, and then added, "It makes me think, Elsa, of your grandmother during the worst days of the Hunger Winter, and of my father, flying in that Big Box formation. Watching his buddies being shot out of the sky. They must have thought as well that it would never end, or that it would only end in catastrophe for them: your grandma and my father. And your great-grandmother, her husband in effect starving himself to death so that she might live, and my Riley grandparents, one son dead in the Pacific, and the other whom they were told was badly burned and crippled. They must have thought that 'it would never end.' And then, your mother, winning through, making a new life for herself, meeting your father, creating you. And my parents, making a good life with one another, bringing a new version of 'The Old Man' into the world. And now you and I come along, from so far apart to become so close together.

So it does end, and each end is a beginning, and each beginning is an end unto itself.

And yet here we are, My Love, here we are."

ELSA (NOVEMBER, 1983)

I knew that I was hanging on, not by a thread, not yet, but hanging on; measuring my waning personal reserves against the cumulative weight of the daily ordeal. In truth, I loved Saint Luke, loved putting my intellect and moral and physical strength against the daily challenges, always the same, and always different. I would actually count, each evening, my wins and losses.

I began to understand that I was a fighter: tenacious, crafty, passionate about my profession. I took each death, and each survival, personally, to be counted and weighed in the balance. I resolved to fight fearlessly, never giving in, for each child's survival as if it were my own. My own survival, not the child's.

And I realized, of course, that this was my weakness as well as my strength. The drain on my physical reserves, and even on my psyche, was enormous, and far from healthy. Without Jake, and the deep bond cemented between us, and the capacity for our laughter, and the sweetness of our nights together, without these I knew I would never be able to make it.

As October began, I, as did others, recovered a bit of lost ground, or at least decreased the pace of losing ground, as the immediate shock of the killings retreated into dreams and memory. A big boost in morale for me came when Sister Marlene announced that the Italians had located a Pediatrician who would be available in December, at least for six months, and also that Canada Child Survival had been able to engage a married couple for a year's commitment: she was a General Surgeon, and he was an Internist with a specialty in infectious disease. He was American, she was Canadian, and they had been serving with the U.S Indian Health Service at the teaching hospital in Gallup, New Mexico. They would arrive at Saint Luke in early Spring.

Along with the wave of relief, part of me said to the other part of me, "How can someone take my place? This is MY place." And then I felt a greater wave of shame, at my selfishness and arrogance, even though unconscious.

And then, in October, the measles came.

The Relief Camp was crowded with more families, in more crowded conditions. Groups of refugees traveling together seemed to be in larger and larger bunches, and their nutritional status was markedly worse. Of course, Ethiopia was now at the point of the third year in a row of failed harvests, rather than somewhere in the middle of the second year. The cumulative effects of less food and more social chaos was manifesting itself.

I had not seen a case of measles for a couple of months; there had been a trickle in the early summer, but then, perhaps surprisingly, nothing since.

But now it was as if a floodgate had opened. The usual pattern of measles in African children was in marked difference to the primary school age it had been in North America: in Africa it was a disease of the end of the first year of life, and of the second and third years. Ethiopian, and in general, African, infants and small children are not as isolated from other children as they are in the West until they attend preschool and then elementary school. African mothers are always socially clustered with other African mothers, drawing water, gathering firewood, cooking around a common pot. And their babies are in close contact with other babies, being carried slung around the mother's back or at her breast. And, without access to the highly-effective measles vaccine, which was not available in most of Ethiopia at this time, and certainly not in the rural areas, and most certainly not among the famine refugees on the move, contagion among the infants and young children was ubiquitous. So, as opposed to North America, where pre-vaccination measles was largely a disease of well-nourished school-age children, measles in Ethiopia, and in most of Africa, was a disease of infants and very young children, usually just at the age when malnutrition was most prevalent and most severe. The Ethiopian famine magnified these effects in a major way.

Measles is among the most contagious of known childhood infections. I had learned in medical school that, before the wide availability of the vaccine in the 1960's, if one child on a school bus was in the infectious stage of early illness (and before the appearance of the characteristic rash), every other child on that bus, except for those who had already experienced the disease, would become infected. So I could well think of the Relief Camp, and the traveling groups of refugees, as 'large school buses' full of very vulnerable children.

But the problem of high prevalence of the disease at Saint Luke was only the first part of the story. There is no direct specific therapy for measles, but measles can be accompanied by severe pneumonia, blindness (especially in Vitamin A-deficient children), deafness, cerebral involvement. These outcomes are much more frequent when an infant or child is malnourished, with an impaired immune system, or with other additional medical conditions, such as anemia, or concurrent other infections.

And that, in turn, is only the second part of the story. After a course of the disease itself, with its fever, inanition, and usually reduced food intake, the poorly-nourished child may survive the measles itself, only to fall precipitously, several days or weeks after 'recovery from measles', into a profound state of kwashiorkor or marasmus, and then expire, not of 'measles', but of malnutrition.

This is what happened at Saint Luke, and, in effect, across most of central and northern Ethiopia in the autumn of 1983. It was like a wildfire in a dry cornfield. It swept from the famine borderlands into the Relief Camp, and into and through my outpatient and inpatient service

Soon the inpatient capacity was exhausted. Jake helped organize another separate tent, for measles cases only. Within a week, it was filled to capacity, 20, 30 cases or more. In the early stages of the disease, children's eyes are painfully sensitive to light. So the problem arose, how to reduce the light in the tent without cutting down air flow, or allowing the temperature to rise; either or both of which would make the situation of the patients worse.

Jake, with some cutting and fitting, was able to alter the 'measles tent' so that there was a light-screened aperture at the tent peak, and semi light-dimming of the flap door and windows. He was also able to scavenge two small electric fans and a string of long extension cords from somewhere in Addis, with which to improve circulation air inside the tent, but, since power was only available a few short hours a day, this effect was limited. We appreciated the darkness of night. And, as we had learned by sad experience, the hospital drain on electricity from surgery, lighting, x-ray, water pumps, and other critical power needs, made the 'non-system system' highly susceptible to outages. Jake worked out a complex schedule, approved by Sister Marlene, for the most efficient time-distribution of power, among the hospital's various needs. Not something I had learned much about in medical school in Toronto.

The tidal wave of measles began, as I looked back on it, with a few cases in late September. It rose, slowly at first, to a crescendo by mid-October. Then, it slowly diminished, so that by early November, there were only a trickle, and now a near-absence of fresh cases of measles.

And, just as we were drawing breath, many of the 'recovered' measles patients began to return, with severe and acute kwashiorkor, or marasmus, accompanied by severe diarrhea or pneumonia.

Between 15 and 20 percent of my acute measles patients had not survived. Of those 'recovered' and discharged, almost 10 percent were re-admitted in the following weeks for severe malnutrition or infection. Of these, almost another 20 percent did not survive. Had we not been able, back in the Spring, a program of nutritional recovery for severely malnourished children, involving the mothers themselves in preparation of high-value feedings, many more of these children would have perished. I wonder where each of them are today.

Much of October is only a blur in my memory, or rather the general situation remains as a blur; there are also a multitude of sharply-focused and never-to-be-forgotten specific cases and incidents.

All of us: me, Asfaw, the Nursing Sisters, and the Nursing Assistants and the cooks and cleaners, and the sweepers and the laundry people—we just worked around the clock and the calendar, stopping only for a few hours' rest when exhausted. Jake worked the same way on the days and nights he could be down here. There were few more evening walks. Jake and I just dropped, husked out, onto the doubled cots, clung together, slept like the dead for a few hours, got up, and did it all over again.

One night, near the end of October, Jake shook me awake about 3 a.m. "Are you OK?" He explained to me (I was so groggy I hardly heard him), "Elsa, you sat up like a shot, appearing wide awake while still asleep, tears running down your face, and you shouted, 'Jake, Jake, what if we had had vaccine, Jake? What if we had had vaccine?' Then you flopped down like a rag doll and closed your eyes again."

JAKE (NOVEMBER, 1983)

I realized that, following the measles outbreak, and those deaths, and the trail of malnutrition deaths that followed it, Elsa had not really recovered, neither physically or mentally, and that she was near, or at, her breaking point, like some of the soldiers I had seen in Nam. Of course, in addition to the 'measles-related' illness and deaths, the 'regular load' had to be carried on. And the loss of Dr. Gennari, with no surgical replacement yet arrived, added immeasurably to the physical and psychological strain. Sister Marlene was now 'the' surgeon, in addition to her ob/gyn and administrative duties. Surgery was cut back to the absolutely necessary, and this itself added to the stress and care burdens. Elsa, and Asfaw were pulled in to do what 'minor' surgery needed to be done, and to assist Sister Marlene with major caes, and this, in turn, increased the spiral throughout the various medical, pediatric, and surgical practice.

Everyone was exhausted as that spiral continued to tighten, and even increased with the failure of the year's harvest, and a further increase of refugees to the Relief Camp and the hospital.

Frankly, I don't know how they did it, how they maintained not only their endurance but also their balance. I had seen a few cases of 'combat fatigue', or PTSD, in Nam, and this was very much on my mind, especially with regard to Elsa. I tried to help where and when I could, and the CSS management were very understanding and, where possible, lightened my driving load, but I just did not have in any real sense the skills that were required.

For the first time in my life, I knew the feelings of deep inadequacy.

Elsa became less communicative, even with me. She still carried on her full schedule with Asfaw and the Nursing Assistants, not flagging in her work, but she walked now rather than scurried, and her head was down, pointing at the ground. Asfaw took on more and more of organizing and directing things. Elsa, though she could not admit it to me, or even to herself, began to look more and more forward to the end of each day, and to the arrival of the 'new' Pediatrician, by report an Italian woman with significant prior experience working in Somalia.

The turning point came two evenings ago, when Elsa and I were sitting quietly on the 'cushionless sofa', the sky almost as bright as daylight under a full moon. We were talking of how a country could be so beautiful and so wondrous, and so horrific and terrifying, all at the same time.

I noticed the change in Elsa's breathing, as her chest expanded and contracted as she rested against my shoulder. She would take a short, almost staccato breath in, then hold it for a moment longer than usual, then a shorter and more abrupt breath out, hold again... and then repeat the process.

I could see that Elsa's eyes were full of tears, though there was no sound of weeping, and that she was biting her lower lip.

And then I saw that her left hand was trembling, and her thumb began to unconsciously rub back and forth, back and forth, along her forefinger. Her mouth hung half-opened, and her eyes stared nowhere and at nothing.

I put my arm around her trembling shoulder, and said, as gently as I could, "My Love, it is time to go."

She gathered herself and replied, "Yes, Jake, it IS time to go. But, please, together?"

I said what was in my heart, "Of course, of course, always, always. Together."

I had the ring ready. I reached into my pocket with my right hand and produced it. It was an ancient Ethiopian band, perhaps from Harar, perhaps from Somalia, perhaps even from far away across the Arabian sea—a band of beaten silver, with tiny stones of unknown colors set gleaming all around the band.

I had the ring from an aged and toothless beggar, who was straggling his way on a rocky stretch of desert road between Harar and Jijiga when I stopped my truck to pick him up. He had only one torn sandal, and The Old Man would stop every fifty yards or so, and switch the sandal to his other foot, and then carry on.

I helped him up the high step, and we sat like that for a while as we shared my water bottle and my wrapped sandwich. Then I restarted the motor, and we moved on, towards Jijiga.

A ways on, in the middle of nowhere, he signed that he needed to get off. I stopped the truck, and before he left me, walking off into nowhere with his face turned to the west, we said goodbye in that African Muslim way: a light quick handshake, then your right hand reaching up to touch against, first your heart, and then your forehead.

The Old Man reached into his robe, withdrew the ring, and gave it to me.

As he hobbled off into the desert, wearing a well-used pair of size 11 running shoes (I could always get another pair in the bazaar in Harrar, if not in Jijiga), The Old Man turned his face to me and said, in fractured Amharic:

"The ring will bring you Happiness. "

And so it has, so it has.

Elsa and I and Ethiopia had come full circle. When I placed the ring on her finger, I recited to her the poem that had always been my favorite, written by Edward Lear, a short decade after Matthew Riley was born. The poem the Farmer's Wife had taught The Old Man, my grandfather, to read by. The poem the brave and lonely boy had brought with him to America. The poem Matthew Riley taught his Edna, herself a lonely girl come from Who Knew Where. And the poem my Gramma Riley had read, over and over, to me.

And now I was giving it to my Elsa, herself the daughter of an immigrant, and she in her turn would pass it along:

The Owl and the Pussycat went to sea, in a beautiful pea-green boat.

They took some money, and plenty of honey, wrapped up on a five-pound note.

The Owl looked up to the stars above, and sang to a small guitar,

Oh, beautiful Pussy, oh Pussy my Love, what a beautiful Pussy you are, you are,

What a beautiful pussy you are.

Pussy said to the Owl, Oh you elegant fowl, how charmingly sweet you sing,

Come, let us be married, too long have we tarried, but what shall we do for a ring?

They sailed away, for a year and a day, to the land where the Bong tree grows,

And there in a wood, a Piggy-Wig stood, with a ring in the end of his nose, his nose,

With a ring in the end of his nose.

Dear Pig, are you willing to sell, for one shilling, your ring? Said the Piggy, I will.

So they took it away, and were married next day, by the Turkey who lives on the hill.

They dined on mince, and slices of quince, which they ate with a runcible spoon.

And hand in hand, on the edge of the sand, they danced by the light of the Moon, the Moon,

They danced by the light of the Moon.

POSTCRIPT

Dr. Elsa Evans-Riley and Mr. Jake Riley

Take Great Joy in Announcing

The Birth of their Twins:

Christina Betsey Riley, and Matthew John Riley

5 Pounds 11 Ounces, and 6 Pounds 3 Ounces, Respectively

At Saint Francis Hospital, Topeka, Kansas

November 25, 1985

AUTHOR'S NOTE

Fiction is but past or future history, viewed through the distorted lens of the author's eye.

"Famine, War, and Love" was born this way: Decades ago, in the early 1960's, as a medical student, I was wandering in the library, and my eye was caught by a medical journal article on the persistent effects in children of the "Dutch Famine of 1944-5". It kindled an interest that I have followed periodically in the years since, but I learned very little in detail of the Allied food airlift, or of the "Going to the Farms".

A few years ago, a dear friend, LD, showed me an unpublished article, which had been meant, many years ago, for LIFE Magazine, concerning Operation Chowhound and the airlift. The story began to grow in my mind.

For sources, there are a number of excellent books:

Henri A. Van der Zee: "The Hunger Winter: Occupied Holland 1944-1945", Norman and Hobhouse, London, 1982; reprinted by University of Nebraska Press, Lincoln and London, 1998

Tom Bijvoet and Anne van Arragon Hutton, eds: "The Dutch in Wartime: Survivors Remember", Mokeham Publishing, Niagra Falls, NY, 2013. This is a series of 9 small books with short first-person accounts by Dutch citizens. Books 1 (Invasion), 2 (Under Nazi Rule), 3 (Witnessing the Holocaust), 4 (Resisting Nazi Occupation), 8 (The Hunger Winter), and 9 (Liberation), are particularly relevant.

And, in today's world, Wikipedia and You Tube provided a wealth of information, first-hand accounts, references, and graphic photos and news film regarding the Hunger Winter, U.S. WWII air and ground war in Europe, and in particular the B-17 bombers and their crews. Similar extensive background, both in words and film and tape, are web-available regarding the Ethiopian famines of the 1980's.

Most of the medical material in the book comes from my own many years practicing Pediatrics and Community Health in Africa and Asia, a fraction of it in emergency and disaster situations. This work has been both long- and short-term, in hospitals, health centers, and in the bush, including several very brief stints in Ethiopia itself.

Sioux Lookout is described as I experienced it as a *locum tenens* one summer in the 1970's, and I have also drawn on the year I spent at the Grenfell Regional Hospital in Northern Newfoundland in 1981-1982.

The specific settings, including "St. Luke Hospital" are fictional composites, and not meant to be existing places. However, the detail of the story is accurate as I have projected it, as are the locales. There is a statue, standing in a public park in Leeuwarden, Holland, entitled "Woman on a Hunger Trek". The statue depicts a young woman, resolute, eye straight ahead pedaling a bare-tired bicycle, and is unforgettable. I think of Christina that way.

As for the characters, they are mostly entirely fictional, or composites of actual individuals I have known. The courageous Christina, Freddi, and Jacob Vermeer are creatures of my imagination, but their experiences are not. Elsa is a fictional composite of the best Pediatricians that I have had the pleasure and privilege of knowing and working with.

Jacob Riley recalls a little-known and long-deceased uncle of mine, Richard, who served in the Army Air Corps in France, and returned shattered by his experience. Jacob Riley's vision of the line of silent wounded veterans sitting on the VA Hospital veranda, staring at the sun, is an actual scene burned into my own childhood memory one day in 1948 as I passed by such a hospital near New York City.

Matthew Riley, 'The Old Man', was sketched from another favorite long-deceased uncle, not an immigrant, but a True Westerner, born on a Reservation in Oklahoma: cavalryman, gold prospector, and oil field worker. 'Tough but Sweet to the Bone', was my Uncle Mickey Modine.

Jake Riley is who many a boy wants to be. And a good thing that is. An old friend, HP, actually was a long-haul driver for Relief Organizations, but in Kenya rather than Ethiopia.

Sister Marlene embodies for me many medical nuns serving in Africa: their love for humanity, their inner strength and resilience, and their fierce independence of mind and character.

Dr. Gennari, the "Surgeon's Surgeon" is drawn from African and European surgeons that I have known. Their bark is usually accompanied by a very accurate bite.

Asfaw Desta is a composite of the best of my beloved medical students in Cameroun in the early 1970's. They epitomized to me the hopeful future of their country, as did Asfaw.

There are only 2 'true-to-life' characters in the book: Solomon and Anna, who indeed came to this New World from Romania via London, crossing the Atlantic in steerage on the steamer St. Paul. They were my grandparents. And, I am told, Solomon had red hair, just as Matthew observed.

My deep thanks to LD, for his striking of the match, and for his encouragement.

And, for unfailing support, straight talk, and better ideas, I owe a Lover's Debt to my wife, Elizabeth. Lest we forget, her father was among those G.I.'s who built the B-17airfields in the English Midlands, possibly the very base that the Big Chief flew from.

SCJ